# Greenwich and East London
## Step by Step

# Greenwich and East London Step by Step

CHRISTOPHER
TURNER

faber and faber
LONDON · BOSTON

First published in 1986
as part of *Outer London Step by Step*
by Faber and Faber Limited
3 Queen Square London WC1N 3AU
These sections first published
separately with revisions and additions in 1987

Photoset by Parker Typesetting Service Leicester
Printed in Great Britain by
Butler & Tanner Ltd Frome Somerset
All rights reserved

© Christopher Turner 1986, 1987
Drawings © Benoit Jacques 1986, 1987
Maps by Ken Smith

*British Library Cataloguing in Publication Data*

Turner, Christopher, *1934–*
Greenwich and East London Step by Step.
1. Greenwich (London, England:London
Borough)—Description—Guide-books
I. Title
914.21'6204858      DA685.G68
ISBN 0-571-14634-1

# Contents

# Acknowledgements

For their kindness and help I should like to thank the numerous librarians, architects, press officers, church officers, clerks, hoteliers and curators who have advised on and checked the contents of this book. A tremendous amount of valuable time was given by the following in particular: the London Tourist Board, the Historic Buildings and Monuments Commission, the National Maritime Museum and the London Borough of Greenwich.

# Introduction

Much of the charm of the London Borough of Greenwich derives from the stark contrast between its verdant parkland, studded with outstanding historic buildings, and the approach to it through derelict industrial wasteland, uninspired municipal flats and dreary artisans' dwellings.

The excitement engendered by the visual shock of turning the bend in the river and suddenly being confronted by the Baroque 'Queen's View' of the royal buildings is an architectural experience unequalled, certainly in the British Isles, and probably in Europe. Fortunately, the equally outstanding interiors of most of the buildings may also be visited.

Although much of the information in this volume has already appeared in *Outer London Step by Step* (Faber 1986), the East End section, which is also included, has been extended to describe the up to date situation on the important redevelopment of London's old dockland. Moreover, we believe that the Greenwich area, because of its great popularity, also requires this separate volume which will be particularly appreciated by visitors to London with limited time at their disposal.

As with my other books in the *Step by Step* series, I have, throughout, attempted to put myself in the position of a complete stranger who, on arrival, wants to know *exactly* where to go and what route to follow.

Whether on a guided tour or a 'do it yourself' visit, *Greenwich and East London Step by Step* will add immeasurably to your appreciation of this uniquely fascinating London borough. You will know what is open and when, you won't have to 'swot up' English history in advance and, above all, you won't get lost.

Christopher Turner

# Greenwich

The town is visited mainly for its complex of 17C royal buildings which, viewed from the river, provides one of England's best known vistas. The National Maritime Museum, Old Royal Observatory and the Painted Hall and Chapel of the Royal Naval College now occupy much of this complex and can be visited daily throughout the year.

*Timing*  Monday to Saturday is preferable, allowing a whole day to see the town and its museums. The Royal Naval College does not open until 14.30.

*Suggested connections*  Continue to Blackheath, Charlton or Woolwich if time permits.

Special buses connect Greenwich Pier with the Thames Barrier at Woolwich.

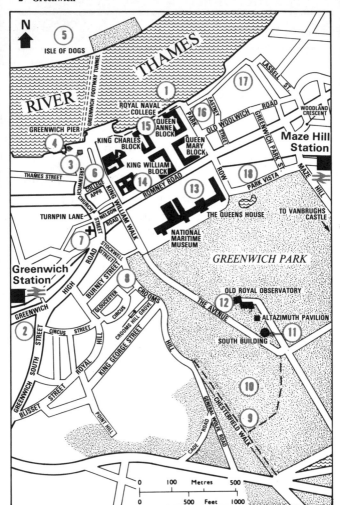

## Locations

**Start** *Greenwich Station (BR) from Charing Cross Station (BR).*

*Alternatively, Greenwich can be reached by river boats, most of which are now almost completely covered. Much of the journey is through London's old dockland but when the tide is right it ends with the world famous riverside view of the royal buildings of Greenwich, 'The Queen's View'.*

*Boats leave Charing Cross Pier (opposite Embankment Station, Bakerloo, Circle, District and Northern Lines) from 10.00 and from Westminster Pier (south of Westminster Station, Circle and District Lines) from 10.30. Calls are made at the Festival Pier and the Tower Pier. Check the time of the last boat if returning by river.*

| Location 1 | **GREENWICH FROM THE RIVER 'THE QUEEN'S VIEW'** |
|---|---|

If a view of the royal buildings is provided from the boat, they are seen as follows:

The buildings, which originally formed the Royal Naval Hospital, but which now house the Royal Naval College (Location 14), are grouped in the foreground.

Directly overlooking the river R is **King Charles Block**.

Behind this lies **King William Block**.

Directly overlooking the river L is **Queen Anne Block**.

Behind this lies **Queen Mary Block**.

The white villa, situated behind this complex in Greenwich Park, is **The Queen's House** which, with its wings linked by the colonnade, houses most of the National Maritime Museum (Location 13).

On the hill, behind R, is the **Old Royal Observatory** (Location 12), now also part of the Maritime Museum.

The large boat R is *Cutty Sark* (Location 3).

The small ketch further R is *Gypsy Moth IV* (Location 4).

•● *From Greenwich Pier proceed ahead to* Cutty Sark (Location 3).

•● *Alternatively, if arriving at Greenwich Station, exit to Greenwich High Road and cross the road to Queen Elizabeth's College.*

| Location 2 | **QUEEN ELIZABETH'S COLLEGE** *James Gibson (?) 1817* |
|---|---|

| Greenwich High Road | The almshouses were founded during the reign of Elizabeth I, *c.*1574, by the historian William Lambarde. They were rebuilt on the same site. |
|---|---|

•● *Continue ahead to Greenwich Church St and proceed to the river. Turn L to* Cutty Sark.

---

| Location 3 | **CUTTY SARK** |

*Open Monday–
Saturday 10.30–17.00.
Sunday 12.00–17.00.
April–September
closes at 18.00.
Admission charge.*

The *Cutty Sark*, which has lain here in dry dock
since 1954, is the last surviving clipper ship. It
was designed in 1869 specifically for the China tea
trade, which required speedy transport, as higher
prices were paid for early deliveries of each new
season's crop. Later, the boat served the
Australian wool trade and remained at sea until
1922. A crew of twenty were needed to control its
30,000 sq ft of rigging. The name *Cutty Sark* was
inspired by the cutty sark (Scottish for a short
linen nightshirt) worn by Nannie, the fastest
witch in Robert Burns's 'Tam O'Shanter'.
Nannie is represented by *Cutty Sark*'s figurehead.

The boat's history is described within, and part of
the world's largest collection of figureheads from
ships' prows is displayed.

*Exit and proceed ahead to* Gipsy Moth IV.

---

| Location 4 | **GIPSY MOTH IV** |

*Open April–October
Monday–Saturday
11.00–18.00.
Sunday 14.30–18.00.
October closes at
17.00. Admission
charge.*

This 54 ft vessel is the ketch in which Sir Francis
Chichester became, at the age of sixty-six, the
first man to sail around the world single-handed.
Chichester commissioned the boat which was
completed in 1966. He took 226 days to complete
the 29,630 mile journey, landing at Greenwich in
1967. Here he was knighted by Elizabeth II with
the same sword that Elizabeth I had used in the
16C to knight Sir Francis Drake, also at
Greenwich.

*Exit L to the domed building. This houses the
lift to the Greenwich Foot Tunnel which leads to
the Isle of Dogs on the north bank of the Thames.*

*Alternatively, proceed southward along King
William Walk to Greenwich town centre,
(Location 6). First R College Approach.*

---

| Location 5 | **THE ISLE OF DOGS** |

The tunnel entails a ¼-mile walk in each
direction. A ferry service has been proposed, due
to the new housing developments, and this would
be a great improvement as the walk is tedious and
the tunnel always cold, even on the hottest day.
However, unless visitors by boat have been
lucky, it is the only way of seeing 'The Queen's
View' during a visit to Greenwich.

At the Isle of Dogs proceed to the public gardens
which overlook the river. The view is described in
Location 1.

It is not certain how the Isle of Dogs gained its
strange name. In the Middle Ages the area was
known as Stepney Marsh. The first known
mention of the Isle of Dogs was made in 1588 and
probably referred to the hunting hounds that
Henry VIII kept on 'the island'.

*Return to Greenwich and proceed past* Cutty
Sark *to Greenwich Pier. R King William Walk.
First R College Approach.*

| Location 6 | **GREENWICH TOWN CENTRE** |
|---|---|

Much of the town centre dates from the improvement scheme designed by *Joseph Kay* in the 1830s. The stucco façades of King William Walk, College Approach, Greenwich Church Street and Nelson Road were part of this scheme. The area that they cover was once the site of the 15C monastic establishment of the Observant Friars, dissolved at the Reformation.

*◖● Continue along College Approach. First L enter the market.*

The right to hold a market was granted to the hospital in 1700. Fruit and vegetables have been sold here, wholesale only, since 1737. The present covered market was built by *Kay* in 1831. Inscribed above the entrance arch, within the market, is the motto 'A false balance is abomination to the Lord but a just weight is his delight.'

*◖● Return to College Approach L. L Greenwich Church Street. Second L (through the arch) Turnpin Lane. Second R King William Walk. First R Nelson Rd. L Greenwich Church St. Cross to St Alfege's Church.*

| Location 7 | **ST ALFEGE** *Hawksmoor 1714* |
|---|---|

Greenwich Church Street (858 6828)

*Generally open by appointment only apart from services.*

St Alfege's is regarded as one of Hawksmoor's finest churches, however, little survives internally from his time; the steeple is by *James*.

St Alfege was a Saxon Archbishop of Canterbury who was kidnapped by the Danes from his cathedral. A rescue bid failed and he was martyred at sea in 1012 for refusing to request a ransom. A 12C church is the first to be recorded here. The roof of the St Alfege that preceded the present building collapsed during a storm in 1710. In that church, Henry VIII had been baptised and Thomas Tallis, the Tudor organist and composer, buried.

The rebuilt body of St Alfege's was the first to be paid for with money allocated under the Fifty New Churches Act of 1711. Initially, the medieval west tower was retained but eventually it was encased by *James* in 1730. His steeple was completely rebuilt in 1813 as a replica.

At the east end, the original railings are punctuated by stone piers, sumounted by urns decorated with cherubs, now rather faded.

*◖● Proceed to the west end and enter the church.*

St Alfege's was gutted by bombs in the Second World War and much was lost.

Little of the original monochrome painting by *Thornhill* in the apse survived apart from that on the pilasters. The remainder has been repainted.

The wrought ironwork is original.

The pulpit is a reproduction.

Undoubtedly the greatest loss was the woodwork by *Gibbons*. However, the carved supports of the Royal Pew in the south aisle survived the conflagration.

Wolfe of Quebec is buried in the crypt.

🡒 *Exit to Greenwich High Rd R. First R Stockwell St leads to Crooms Hill.*

| Location 8 | **CROOMS HILL** |

Crooms Hill is one of London's oldest known roads, 'crom' being a Celtic word for crooked – the road winds uphill around the park. It has always been the most fashionable street in Greenwich and the west side is lined with 17C and 18C houses, some of which incorporate elements from even earlier buildings.

Most of the east side of Crooms Hill is bordered by Greenwich Park. Noteworthy houses, all on the west side, are passed as follows:

**Nos 6–12**, 1721.

**No 14** is mid 18C.

**Nos 16–18**, 1656.

**Nos 22–24** are late 18C.

🡒 *R Gloucester Circus. Proceed ahead and turn L.*

**Gloucester Circus** was built by *Searles* in 1791 but only its southern section was completed.

The north side was added, to a different design, in 1840 but much of this was destroyed by Second World War bombing.

🡒 *Return to Crooms Hill R.*

**No 26** is late 18C.

**No 32** is early 18C with a late-18C south wing.

**Nos 34** and **36** are mid 18C.

🡒 *R* **Crooms Hill Grove**.

The street was developed in 1838. Many ground floor windows have been altered.

🡒 *Return to Crooms Hill R.*

**Nos 42–46** were built in 1818 (Nos 44 and 46, unusually, share a porch).

The **gazebo**, which directly overlooks the pavement, was built in 1672, probably by Wren's assistant *Hooke*. It stands in the garden of The Grange and was commissioned by the Lord Mayor of London, Sir William Hooker. The building is much restored.

**No 52**, **The Grange**, behind its high wall, was built in the mid 17C but fragments of much earlier buildings exist internally. It was formerly known as Paternoster Croft. The west wing was added in the 18C.

**Mays Court**, **Nos 54–60**, *c.*1770, have recently been converted into flats.

**No 66**, **Heath Gate House**, *c.*1630, was known until

recently as The Presbytery. It is an early London example of the Dutch style.

Past the 19C church, Our Lady Star of the Sea, **No 68**, now the **Presbytery**, is late 17C.

**Park Hall** was built by *James* in 1724 who intended it for his own occupancy, but the architect eventually decided to live elsewhere. James Thornhill stayed here for a short time while he completed decorating the Painted Hall at the Royal Naval Hospital nearby.

The north wing was added in 1802 and conversion to flats took place in 1932.

Opposite Park Hall, on the west side of Crooms Hill, lies the **Manor House** built *c.*1695 for Sir Robert Robinson, Lieutenant General of the Royal Naval Hospital.

*• Continue ahead following the footpath.*

Here Crooms Hill becomes Chesterfield Walk which overlooks Blackheath. Passed L is the **White House** built in 1694 but its front was remodelled in the 18C. It was occupied by Elizabeth Lawson, the girl courted unsuccessfully by James Wolfe of Quebec, whose parents lived next door in Macartney House.

The main part of **Macartney House**, directly fronting the path R, is late 17C but this was extended on both sides by *Soane* in 1802. Additional extensions were made later in the 19C. The house is now subdivided into flats.

*• Proceed to the next building, Ranger's House.*

| Location 9 | **RANGER'S HOUSE** |
|---|---|

Chesterfield Walk

*Open daily February–October 10.00–17.00. November–January 10.00–16.00. Admission free.*

This late-17C residence, previously known as Chesterfield House, was occupied by Philip, 4th Lord Chesterfield and it was probably here that he wrote the famous letters to his son.

Wings were added, to the south by *Ware* (?) in 1750, and to the north in the late 18C.

The house became the residence of the Ranger of Greenwich Park in 1815.

*• Enter the hall. Turn R.*

Paintings, mainly by the English School, are exhibited in the first room and the south wing's gallery. The Suffolk Collection of family portraits from Charlton Park, Wiltshire, include a famous series of Jacobean portraits by *William Larkin*.

*• Return to the hall and ascend the stairs.*

On the first floor, the Dolmetsch Collection of Musical Instruments is displayed.

*• From the rear of Ranger's House enter its grounds and proceed directly to Greenwich Park.*

*• Alternatively, if visiting Blackheath, exit and follow the path immediately ahead across the heath. Cross General Wolfe Rd and continue ahead to Shooters Hill Rd R. First L Wat Tylers Rd. First R Dartmouth Hill. The Blackheath itinerary may now be joined at location 7 (page 25).*

| | |
|---|---|
| Location 10 | **GREENWICH PARK** |

*Open dawn–dusk.*

This, the oldest of London's ten royal parks, was first enclosed by Humphrey, Duke of Gloucester, in 1427 and later formed the grounds of Greenwich Palace. Deer were introduced in 1515 and remain in the south-east section. The famous French landscape gardener, *Le Nôtre*, laid out the grounds for Charles II in 1662. However, his work was not entirely successful, mainly due to the fact that he never came to England and could not, therefore, survey the area. The park was walled-in by James I in 1619 and part of this wall survives. Greenwich Park was opened to the public *c.*1705.

●● *Proceed ahead through the rose garden. Bear L and continue north of the tennis courts. Cross the road and proceed to the Greenwich Planetarium which lies ahead behind the trees.*

| | |
|---|---|
| Location 11 | **GREENWICH PLANETARIUM** *1899* |

South Building
Greenwich Park
(858 4422)

*Open during school holidays Monday, Tuesday, Thursday and Friday 15.00. Also some Saturdays in summer 14.30 and 15.30. Planetarium programmes are changed regularly; telephone for details. Admission charge.*

The planetarium is situated in the South Building which is part of the Old Royal Observatory. This was built for astrophysics – the study of the structure and lifecycle of stars and planets. Originally, the building housed two large telescopes which are still in use at the Royal Observatory's present home in Sussex. Surmounting the building is the Thompson Dome, named to commemorate the donor of the telescopes. Famous astronomers and instrument makers are recorded on the exterior of the building.

●● *Continue northward.*

Passed L is the **Altazimuth Pavilion**, added to the observatory in 1898.

●● *Continue ahead to the Old Royal Observatory enclosure L. Enter and turn L to the Great Equatorial Building.*

| | |
|---|---|
| Location 12 | **OLD ROYAL OBSERVATORY** |

Greenwich Park
(858 4422)

*Open Monday–Saturday 10.00–18.00; Sunday 14.00–18.00. April–October closes 17.00. Admission charge. A combined ticket also giving entry to the main buildings of the National Maritime Museum is available.*

The Royal Observatory was founded at Greenwich by Charles II in 1675 for astronomical study expressly intended to aid marine navigation. A by-product of this work was the positioning, at Greenwich, of zero longitude, or the Prime Meridian, which gained universal acceptance in 1884 as the basis for the measurement of time throughout the world. Visitors may straddle the brass strip which represents the Prime Meridian, and thus stand with one foot in the Eastern hemisphere and the other in the Western hemisphere.

Buildings were added to the complex from time to time, until the late 19C, but as the Royal Observatory was moved to the cleaner air of Herstmonceux, Sussex, in 1948, their practical function has almost ended. The Old Royal Observatory now forms an important part of the National Maritime Museum and its historic buildings accommodate many ancient and beautiful instruments which illustrate the development of astronomy and the measurement of time. All exhibits are explained and only a selection are, therefore, described in this book.

**☛** *Proceed northward.*

The buildings are passed from south-east to north-west in reverse chronological order of construction. North-west of the entrance is the domed Great Equatorial Building.

**Great Equatorial Building** *1857*. The building was designed to house the observatory's first large telescope (12¾ in). This was replaced by a 28-in model in 1893 and a new, larger dome was built to accommodate it. Second World War bomb damage led to this dome's demolition but it was rebuilt in 1971 when the original telescope was returned from Herstmonceux.

The Visitor Reception Area now occupies part of the ground floor.

**☛** *Exit L and proceed ahead to the Meridian Building. The exterior of this range is passed on the way to Flamsteed House. Its interior is entered and described later.*

**Meridian Building.** Although this long range appears to be entirely mid-18C work, it was extended or remodelled a number of times over a two-hundred-year period from 1676.

The first short, pedimented section passed was completed in 1855, the second section in 1813 and the central section, through which the Greenwich Meridian now passes, was first built in 1809 although remodelled in 1850.

The position of the Prime Meridian is indicated by a brass strip in the courtyard's floor.

**☛** *Continue ahead.*

The final section of the Meridian Building is the oldest and was completed in 1749 as Bradley's New Observatory. At its western extremity it replaced a small Quadrant House constructed in 1725 for Edmund Halley, the second Astronomer Royal and best remembered for predicting the return of the comet that now bears his name.

**☛** *Turn R and proceed towards the entrance to Flamsteed House.*

**Flamsteed House** *Wren 1675*. The house, together with part of its twin east and west pavilions, marked the commencement of the scheme; ancillary buildings are later additions. It was built to accommodate the first Astronomer Royal, the Rev. Dr John Flamsteed. Previously, Flamsteed had made his astronomical observations from the White Tower in the Tower of London. Wren designed the house 'for the observators' habitation and a little for pompe', but his budget was strictly limited. The foundations of a watch tower, built for Humphrey, Duke of Gloucester, in the 15C, were re-used together with second-hand bricks from Tilbury Fort and wood and metal from the Tower of London.

Externally, the house has changed little. Amusing examples of economy are the 'stone' dressings that decorate the angles; many are really of wood.

A 17C plaque is inserted in the wall L of the entrance.

Surmounting the north-east turret is a pole supporting a red ball. This was erected in 1833 as the world's first visual time signal. Since that year the ball has been hoisted half-way up the pole at 12.55, raised to the top at 12.58 and dropped precisely at 13.00. Thereby, all passing vessels have been able to set and verify the accuracy of their chronometers. Modern time-keeping equipment, of course, now makes this redundant but the tradition is maintained.

●● *Proceed to the north-east* **Summer House,** *immediately R of the door.*

This summer house was built in 1676 and used by Flamsteed as his Solar Observatory. It was enlarged and remodelled in 1773. Set in the wall, R of the entrance, is Halley's tombstone.

The extension to Flamsteed House, facing its entrance, was added in 1794.

●● *Enter* **Flamsteed House.**

The small building that accommodates the entrance and stairwell is original to the house.

●● *Ascend the staircase to the Octagon Room.*

**Octagon Room.** *Wren*, who was himself an astronomer, designed this, then known as the Great Room, for observation purposes, and it was used in this way until 1830. The room, which was opened to the public in 1953, is little changed apart from the painting of the woodwork which was originally undecorated.

Flanking the entrance are replicas of the Tompion 17C clocks used by Flamsteed. Early telescopes are also displayed.

Flamsteed had been required to provide his own instruments and after he died his widow insisted on disposing of them. Unfortunately, all that have been traced are three Tompion clocks.

Paintings of Charles II and James II were hung in this room in the 17C but their whereabouts are now unknown. The painting of James II is modern and based on an illustration of the original. That of Charles II, however, is contemporary.

●● *Descend the west stairs ahead and proceed anti-clockwise.*

**Halley Gallery.** This section was added in 1836 to provide three additional living rooms for George Airy, the seventh Astronomer Royal. Representations of the heavens in the form of spheres, globes, and astrolabes, etc. are exhibited.

**Maskelyne Gallery.** This, together with the adjoining room, was added *c.* 1790 to provide two drawing rooms and a library for the fifth Astronomer Royal, Nevil Maskelyne.

Nocturnal time-keeping instruments and hourglasses are exhibited, together with non-mechanical instruments for measuring time. These include a collection of sundials.

**Nathaniel Bliss Gallery.** Here is displayed the Harrison Chronometer.

*◄● Return to the Halley Gallery and descend the stairs.*

**Spencer Jones Gallery.** This basement room was created in 1911. Exhibits relating to mechanical time-keeping are displayed.

*◄● Ascend the stairs. Turn L and proceed first L to the ground floor of Flamsteed House.*

**Seventeenth-century living rooms.** The furniture, although not original to the house, is contemporary with Flamsteed's period. These rooms provided domestic accommodation for the Astronomer Royal until 1948.

*◄● Exit from Flamsteed House R. Follow the railings and proceed through the Upper Garden to Flamsteed's Observatory L.*

**Flamsteed's Observatory.** This was originally built by *Wren* in 1676 at the same time as Flamsteed House. Some original brickwork survives but most has been rebuilt.

From here Flamsteed measured the position of the stars and planets – regarded as his most important work.

*◄● Enter the building which is now divided into two rooms.*

**Quadrant House.** A modern engraving of Flamsteed's 7 ft mural arc, his fundamental measuring instrument, is displayed.

**Sextant House.** Flamsteed's 7 ft equatorial sextant is represented by a full-size working model.

*◄● Proceed from Flamsteed's Observatory to the Meridian Building with which it links.*

**Quadrant Room.** First built by Halley in 1725, this was rebuilt and incorporated in Bradley's New Observatory in 1749. The remainder of this observatory now forms the next two rooms. Two 18C quadrants and Bradley's zenith sector telescope are displayed.

**Middle Room.** This was designed as a work room, with bedroom above (now an office), for Bradley's assistant. Halley's and Bradley's 18C transit instruments are mounted in this room. The latter was brought from Bradley's Transit Room, seen next, where it had been used to define the Greenwich Meridian from 1750 to 1816.

**Bradley's Transit Room.** Troughton's instrument, which replaced Bradley's in 1816, is displayed. It was used to define the Greenwich Meridian which continued to pass through this room until 1850.

**Airy's Transit Circle Room.** The room was built in 1809 but remodelled in 1850 to accommodate Airy's transit circle which, in 1852, replaced Bradley's transit instrument. The Greenwich Meridian was immediately moved 19 ft eastward to pass, as it still does, through this room.

The Greenwich Meridian, or zero degrees longitude, was established by defining an imaginary north–south line across the earth's surface.

Although seamen had used the Greenwich Meridian since 1767 to establish longitudinal positions, the measurement of time varied throughout the world in a haphazard manner. The railways led to the acceptance throughout Great Britain, of Greenwich Mean Time in the 1840s and local British variations then disappeared.

In 1884 the Greenwich Meridian was chosen as the world's Prime Meridian, mainly because most shipping was using charts with Greenwich measurements, and the North American railways based their time zones on Greenwich Mean Time. From 1884, therefore, longitudinal positions were fixed from Greenwich and time zones established throughout the world.

Airy's transit circle is still mounted in this room, although the last of more than 750,000 regular observations was made on it in 1954.

*◄● Proceed through to Museum Shop (exit on to courtyard) and upstairs to Dyson Gallery.*

**Dyson Gallery.** The Museum's collection of historic telescopes are displayed here including instruments used by William Herschel, discoverer of the planet Uranus.

*◄● Ascend stairs to dome of Great Equatorial Building to see 28in telescope, the largest refracting telescope in the UK (see above).*

*◄● Descend spiral staircase from observatory dome and leave Great Equatorial Building. Turn L and exit from the Old Royal Observatory via main gate. The Shepherd Clock is fixed R.*

**Shepherd Clock.** This 24-hour clock is permanently fixed at Greenwich Mean Time and is, therefore, one hour in advance of the time used throughout Britain in summer. It was erected in 1851 and was an early example of an electrically operated public clock.

**Standards of Length.** Below the clock are standard measurements of Imperial lengths. They were fixed here for public use in 1866.

*◄● Return eastward and proceed ahead to the Avenue.*

The statue of Wolfe by *Tait McKenzie*, 1930, was presented to Greenwich by the Canadian government.

Overlooking the east side of the park, in Maze Hill, is Vanbrugh Castle. Its green spire may be seen above the trees. Architect and playwright *Sir John Vanbrugh* designed this house in 1719 in the style of a medieval castle for his own occupancy and lived there until 1726. He also built other 'medieval' dwellings for his family on the same 12-acre site but none of these survives.

•● *Descend the hill R of Queen's House to Park Row. Enter L the East Wing of the National Maritime Museum.*

---

Location 13

**THE QUEEN'S HOUSE AND THE NATIONAL MARITIME MUSEUM**

Greenwich Park (858 4422)

*Open Monday–Saturday 10.00–18.00, Sunday 14.00–18.00. April–October. Winter closes 17.00. Admission charge.*

*NB: The Queen's House is closed for renovation until 1989 at the earliest.*

The Queen's House, designed for Anne of Denmark by *Inigo Jones* in 1616, was England's first Classical building. It forms part of the National Maritime Museum, the world's largest and most important naval museum. Not only the Royal Navy but the entire shipping industry is dealt with.

**East Wing.** This, together with the west wing, seen later, was built by *Alexander* in 1807 to provide a naval boarding school. Almost 1000 boys and girls were accommodated. The school moved in 1933 and this wing became part of the National Maritime Museum when it opened in 1937.

The East Wing is closed for refurbishment until 1988 when it will reopen with a major exhibition 'Armada 1588–1988'. The Wing will then become the location for future special exhibitions.

•● *Exit from the East Wing R and proceed beneath the colonnade towards the Queen's House.*

The colonnade was built by *Alexander* in 1811 to link both wings with the Queen's House.

**The Queen's House** was England's first building to be designed entirely in the Classical style and is, therefore, of major architectural importance. It occupies the site of a lodge gate that straddled the main east to west public road, which originally bisected the grounds of Greenwich Palace. Traditionally, it was at this lodge gate that Walter Ralegh gained a knighthood by laying his cloak on the muddy road for Elizabeth I to walk on.

James I gave Greenwich to his consort, Anne of Denmark, in 1613, possibly as some compensation for his perpetual mistreatment of her, and *Inigo Jones* was commissioned to design a new house for the Queen in 1616. The architect had recently returned from his second visit to Italy, where he had been greatly impressed by the work of Palladio, and was determined to produce, for the first time in England, a Classical Italian villa in Palladian style.

Strangely, he designed two parallel blocks, north and south of the road, which were connected at first floor level by a bridge room, thus repeating the function of the old lodge gate which had linked both sections of the royal estate in a similar way. Anne of Denmark died in 1619, and work ceased with only the ground floor built. The structure was covered with thatch for weather protection until 1629 when Charles I asked Jones to complete the Queen's House for his consort, Henrietta Maria. She became its first occupant *c.*1637.

The visual contrast between the Gothic buildings of the royal palace on the riverside below and the new Classical villa was enormous. The Queen's House soon became known as the White House and later, House of Delight. On her return to England following the Restoration, Henrietta Maria, now the Dowager Queen, once more occupied the Queen's House. Accommodation was increased for her by adding further bridge rooms on either side of the first, *Webb* 1662, and this is why, externally, the house now appears to be a square villa.

From 1688 the residence was occupied, at various times, by the Ranger of Greenwich Park and the Governor of The Royal Hospital. The main road bisecting the house was diverted further north to its present position in 1699 by Lord Romney who was the Ranger at the time. It is still called the Romney Road. Staff of the naval school occupied the house from 1816 until the school moved elsewhere in 1933. The Queen's House was restored and opened to the public as the centrepiece of the National Maritime Museum in 1937.

Externally, the entire upper floor was initially of painted brick, cement rendering being added later.

All the windows were originally casement, but in the 18C the usual conversion to sash took place and those on the ground floor were deepened.

The south façade has a first floor loggia which evokes Washington's White House.

The main feature of the north-river façade is the dual staircase which leads, via a terrace, to the original main entrance from the palace, now a window.

The Queen's House was closed in 1985 for lengthy renovation and its contents will be changed. None of the original furnishings have survived, nor do any of Inigo Jones's chimney-pieces remain *in situ*.

The house will be entered from basement level.

**Great Hall.** The hall is designed as a 40 ft cube, a favourite device of the Palladians. The carved and gilded ceiling beams originally enclosed nine panels painted by *Orazio Gentileschi,* possibly assisted by his daughter, *Artemesia*. These were eventually cut down and erected at Marlborough House, where they remain, for Sarah, Duchess of Marlborough. Apparently, Queen Anne, then still the Duchess's great friend, as the famous quarrel was still to come, gave permission for this vandalism.

The marble floor, designed by *Stone* in 1637, repeats the ceiling pattern.

*•● Leave the hall by the door immediately R of the entrance and ascend the staircase.*

**'Tulip' Staircase.** Designed by *Inigo Jones,* this was Britain's first cantilevered spiral staircase. Its balustrade's pattern, in fact, represents fleur-delys, not tulips, probably as a compliment to Henrietta Maria who was French.

●● *At the first floor turn R. The first door R leads to the North-east Cabinet.*

**Room 6 North-east Cabinet.** This became the King's Presence Chamber for Charles II at the Restoration in 1660.

The ceiling frieze is original and incorporates the monogram of Charles I and Henrietta Maria.

●● *Exit R and follow the gallery to the first door R which leads to the second most important room, the Queen's Bedroom, Room 18.*

**Room 18 Queen's Bedroom.** The bedroom, the most richly decorated room in the house, was converted to provide the Queen's Presence Chamber in 1660; its ceiling's cove retains the original painting. Although the main section was repainted as the original work had been removed during the Commonwealth.

**Rooms 8**, east side, and **10**, west side, are the new bridge rooms added by *Webb* in 1662. Their plaster ceilings are the work of *John Groves*.

●● *Descend the stairs to the ground floor's south range. Proceed through the Orangery to the* **'Van de Velde's Room'.**

Charles II provided a room for use as a studio by the great Dutch maritime painters, father and son, between 1675–78. It is not certain, however, that this was the room assigned to them.

●● *Exit from the Queen's House L and follow the colonnade to the west central wing.*

Like the east wing, already seen, the **west central wing** was added to accommodate the naval school by *Alexander c.*1816. Situated immediately R is the main **bookshop** of the museum.

●● *Continue ahead to the display of seals L and medals R. Return through the bookshop, turn R and proceed to the* **west wings**. *Descend the stairs ahead R to the* **Neptune Hall** *(Lower ground floor, Room H).*

This was built to provide the school's gymnasium and assembly hall in 1874.

Development of the steamship is the theme. The tug *Reliant*, built in 1907 and operational until 1968, is kept in working order and is believed to be the largest item of industrial history exhibited under cover in a European museum.

A cabin from the luxury liner *Empress of Canada* has been reconstructed.

●● *Descend the steps L to the* **Barge House** *(Lower ground floor, Room 6).*

Two royal barges are exhibited including the state barge of Frederick, Prince of Wales, designed by *Kent* in 1732. Beneath its roof is the Prince's coat of arms. This barge was last used by Prince Albert in 1849.

●● *Continue ahead and turn L.*

Lower ground floor, **Rooms B–F** display the development of wooden ships.

☛ *Return to the main staircase and ascend to the first floor.*

**Room E** on the first floor houses Discovery and Seapower 1450–1700, a new gallery exploring the rise of Britain as a world power. Further new galleries on the first floor will open in 1987 (The Development of the Warship 1650–1810) and 1988.

**Room F** is a Special Exhibition Gallery.

☛ *Descend to the mezzanine floor and proceed to Rooms A–E.*

Captain Cook's discovery of New Zealand is featured in **Room A**.

Nelson's naval career is dealt with in **Room E**. Displayed is 'The Battle of Trafalgar' painted by *Turner*.

Opposite this is the coat worn by Nelson at Trafalgar, clearly showing the hole made by the fatal bullet.

☛ *Return through Room E and proceed to the* **south-west wing**.

This building was added by *Pasley* in 1876. It will hold temporary exhibitions throughout 1987.

☛ *Leave the museum from the north side of the west wing. L Romney Rd. First R King William Walk. Enter the Royal Naval College R.*

---

Location 14

King William Walk
(858 2154)

*Open Friday–
Wednesday 14.30–
17.00. Thursday
closes at 16.45.
Admission free.*

## ROYAL NAVAL COLLEGE

The buildings that now form the college provide England's most important complex in the Classical style. Although mainly designed by *Wren* for William and Mary as a naval hospital, it was the earlier design by *Webb* of King Charles Block, part of a projected palace for Charles II, that set the style for the whole scheme.

The college covers much of the site once occupied by Greenwich Palace. Internally, only the Painted Hall and Chapel may be visited.

**The Plantagenet and Tudor Palace.** Bella Court, a medieval manor house, was erected on the site of an abbot's residence built in Saxon times. It was inherited by Humphrey, Duke of Gloucester in 1426, who transformed it into a fortified castle.

Margaret of Anjou, consort of Henry VI, acquired the property in 1447. She embellished the house which was renamed Pleasaunce and later Placentia. It became the favourite residence of the Tudors, being much rebuilt by Henry VII and extended by Henry VIII who married Catherine of Aragon and Anne of Cleves within its chapel. Henry VIII, Mary I and Elizabeth I were born at the palace. Only a fragment of the complex remains. (see Location 18, The Chantry).

**Stuart Buildings.** James I is believed to have constructed the undercroft beneath the Great Hall *c.*1605 and this is the oldest part of the actual palace to survive. It is no longer open to the public.

Greenwich Palace was vandalized by Cromwell, and at the Restoration Charles II instigated a grand rebuilding scheme. As a first step, the east section of King's House (now King Charles Block) was constructed by *Webb* in 1664. However, the King lost interest, money ran out and work ceased. James II, during his brief reign, carried out no further work. William and Mary preferred to reside at Kensington Palace or Hampton Court and the concept of a new Greenwich Palace was doomed.

Following the naval victory over the French in 1692, Mary II ordered building to recommence and *Wren* was commissioned in 1694 to provide, not a palace, but the Royal Naval Hospital for elderly and wounded seamen, a plan first conceived by Mary's father, James II. A Royal Hospital had opened at Chelsea in 1692, also designed by *Wren*, to serve the needs of soldiers in a similar way.

At Greenwich, as at Chelsea, Wren wanted to provide an unbroken river façade, but Mary would not allow the recently opened-up view of the river from The Queen's House to be obstructed again, nor would she allow the existing King's House, built for her uncle, Charles II, to be altered. This is why The Queen's House, although small and rather distant, surprisingly forms the axis of this grand Baroque design. During the construction of the hospital, all the existing palace buildings, apart from King's House and an undercroft, were demolished. Although the first pensioners were accommodated by 1705, construction work continued for another fifty years with *Hawksmoor*, and later *Vanbrugh*, as surveyors. By 1869 the number of pensioners had decreased from the original 30,000 to 15,000 and it was then decided to provide them with funds to support themselves. The Royal Naval College transferred here from Portsmouth in 1873 and still occupies the building.

●● *Proceed ahead passing L an early-19C single storey range.*

Ahead L is the **King Charles Block**. Its west façade was rebuilt by *Yenn* in 1814 following a fire.

Only the eastern half of the south façade is by *Webb*.

*Wren* built the western half mirroring Webb's design. This section, however, was rebuilt as a replica by *J. Stuart* in 1769.

The **King William Block**'s west façade R was built, mainly for economic reasons, in red brick, probably by *Hawksmoor* in 1702. Such a flamboyant design is unlikely to have been the work of Wren.

Its north façade was completed by *Wren* in 1705.

Immediately L is the long east façade of the **King Charles Block**, all the work of *Webb*. This set the style for the whole scheme when it was built in 1629 as the first stage of Charles II's royal palace that was never to materialize.

Opposite, stands the **Queen Anne Block**, designed by *Wren* as a replica of the King Charles Block. This was completed in 1725.

●● *Ascend the steps.*

The **Queen Mary Block** ahead was also designed by *Wren* but not completed until 1751.

●● *Turn R and enter the King William Block's Painted Hall R.*

**Painted Hall.** This is divided into three sections: vestibule, great hall and upper hall. Its interior decoration was completed by *Hawksmoor* in 1707. *Thornhill* began the painting of the ceiling and walls in 1708 but he did not complete the work until 1727. During the building of this block William III, Anne and George I reigned successively and they are all featured in the paintings.

**Vestibule.** Situated directly beneath the cupola, this was the last part of the hall to be decorated. Paintings on the dome represent the four winds.

Names of the hospital's benefactors are painted on the walls.

●● *Ascend the steps.*

**Great Hall.** Nelson lay in state here in 1805 prior to his funeral in St Paul's Cathedral. The allegorical ceiling, completed in 1713, depicts William and Mary providing Europe with its freedom. It is judged to be the greatest Baroque painting by a British artist.

Mirrors on trolleys assist viewing of the ceiling.

●● *Ascend the steps to the Upper Hall.*

**Upper Hall.** The ceiling painting features Queen Anne and her consort, Prince George of Denmark.

On the wall immediately ahead George I is depicted with his family. Much of this painting is the work of *Andre,* Thornhill's collaborator. In the foreground *Thornhill* has painted himself beckoning to the onlooker.

The monochrome side walls illustrate the landing at Greenwich of William III (R) and George I (L).

From the windows can be seen the only view permitted of the east façade of this block. It is the most idiosyncratic work at Greenwich and again probably by *Hawksmoor*.

●● *Exit from the Painted Hall and cross the courtyard ahead to the Queen Mary Block. Enter the Chapel.*

**Chapel.** The interior, completed in 1742, was almost entirely destroyed by fire in 1779 and rebuilt ten years later by *James (Athenian) Stuart* in the Greek style. Much of the detail, however, was designed by the clerk of works *William Newton*.

The carving above the doorway is by *Bacon*.

•● *Enter the vestibule.*

The four Coade stone statues were designed by *West*.

Originally, the pulpit formed the top section of a three-decker. Its medallions by *West* illustrate scenes from the life of St Paul.

The present altar rail was made in 1787.

Above the altar is a painting of St Paul's shipwreck by *West*.

•● *Exit from the chapel and return to King William Walk R. At Greenwich Pier follow the riverside path R.*

If the 'Queen's View' of the royal buildings has not been seen, the nearest equivalent can be viewed from this path as described in Location 1.

•● *Continue ahead. Behind the railings is the central lawn of the college with its statue of George II.*

| Location 15 | **GEORGE II MONUMENT** *Rysbrack 1735* |
|---|---|

The King is fashionably depicted wearing a Roman toga. Marble used for the monument was allegedly discovered in a captured French ship.

•● *Proceed ahead and pass the college buildings.*

| Location 16 | **THE TRAFALGAR TAVERN** |
|---|---|

Built in Regency style by *Kay* in 1837, the tavern replaced the Old George, an 18C inn. The Trafalgar was once famed for its dinners of whitebait, a small fish caught in the Thames during summer. These dinners were favoured by members of Parliament, and the entire Cabinet boated regularly to the Trafalgar for the feast. Names of those who participated in the more notable dinners are listed on boards which line the walls of the upper banqueting room. River pollution ended the catches and the whitebait dinners. The inn went into decline and closed in 1915. Although earmarked for redevelopment, the Trafalgar survived, and was refurbished and re-opened in 1968.

Whitebait dinners have been resumed, but the catch is no longer fresh from the Thames.

•● *Exit L. Follow the path first L (Crane St) and continue ahead passing the Yacht Tavern L. Immediately R is Trinity Hospital. (If an appointment has been made, the chapel is entered by ringing the entry bell R of the first gate R.)*

| Location 17 | **TRINITY HOSPITAL** |
|---|---|

Ballast Quay

*Open free by appointment only. Apply to the Warden.*

The hospital was founded as almshouses by Henry Howard, Earl of Northampton in 1613. As the Earl was born in Norfolk it was stipulated that eight of the pensioners accommodated should always come from that county and the hospital became known as Norfolk College. It was much restored c.1812 when battlements and the rendering were added.

The chapel was completely rebuilt in 1812.

Outside the chapel stand figures of the Virtues, allegedly the earliest known English reproductions of antique originals.

•● *Enter the* **chapel**.

Above the altar is an early-16C Flemish stained glass window.

Below the south window R is the monument to Henry Howard by *Stone*, c.1696. Its tracery is a notably early example of Neo-Gothic work. The effigy was brought here from Dover Castle by the Mercers Company in 1696 but the original canopy has been lost.

•● *Exit R and proceed to the* **Cutty Sark** *inn*.

This was built in 1804 and its huge bow window is original.

•● *Exit L. First L Lassell St. Continue ahead and cross the main road to Woodland Crescent. L Maze Hill. First R Park Vista.*

| Location 18 | **PARK VISTA** |
|---|---|

The road contains many properties of interest. Most of the south side fronts Greenwich Park.

**Nos 1–11** are early 19C.

**No 13**, **Manor House**, has an early 18C front with a later gazebo on the roof.

**No 15**, **Hamilton House**, is mid 18C.

**Nos 16–18**, **Park Place**, are dated 1791.

Of greatest interest is **The Chantry**, on the south side backing the park, as it retains vestiges of an outbuilding of Greenwich Palace. Lying back, at upper level, is some 16C brickwork to which is fixed a modern stone replica of Tudor arms.

•● *Return to Maze Hill R and proceed southward to view Vanbrugh's Castle more closely.*

•● *Alternatively, return to Maze Hill L. First R Tom Smith Close and Maze Hill Station (BR) to Charing Cross Station (BR).*

•● *Alternatively, if continuing to Charlton, train to Charlton Station (BR).*

•● *Alternatively, if continuing to Woolwich, train to Woolwich Arsenal Station (BR).*

# Blackheath

Blackheath grew around its heath and the 'village', which lies to the south, was a later development. Many outstanding period buildings survive, including The Paragon, one of the country's finest late-18C crescents, and Pagoda House, probably the most eccentric residence in the London area.

*Timing*  Any day is suitable, but fine weather is essential as only Morden College may be entered (by appointment).

*Suggested connections*  Precede with Greenwich (part). Continue to Charlton or Greenwich (part).

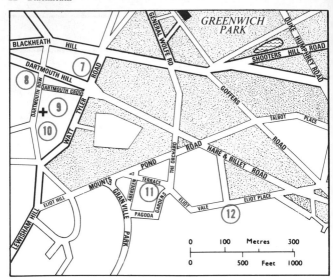

*Locations*
1  Blackheath 'Village'
2  Montpelier Row
3  Blackheath
4  South Row
5  The Paragon
6  Morden College
7  Dartmouth Hill
8  Dartmouth Row
9  Church of the Ascension
10  Dartmouth House
11  Pagoda House
12  Eliot Place
13  Grotes Buildings
14  Lloyds Place
15  Tranquil Vale

**Start** *Blackheath Station (BR) from Charing Cross Station (BR). Exit from the station L Tranquil Vale.*

*Alternatively, continue from Greenwich as indicated, beginning at Dartmouth Hill, location 7.*

| Location 1 | **BLACKHEATH 'VILLAGE'** |
|---|---|
| | Tranquil Vale, together with its southern extension named Blackheath Village, forms the centre of what is now referred to as 'the village', but the importance of this southern end of the thoroughfare was only established in the 19C with the coming of the railway. Blackheath first developed further north, around the heath, and this is where the oldest buildings survive. |
| | ◆➤ *First R Montpelier Vale leads to Montpelier Row.* |
| Location 2 | **MONTPELIER ROW** |
| | Montpelier Row, which leads to the heath, was developed in the late 18C and early 19C. |
| | ◆➤ *First R South Row. Immediately L is Blackheath.* |
| Location 3 | **BLACKHEATH** |
| | The heath has long been public, but is now traversed by numerous roads, many of which were laid out in the 19C and 20C. |

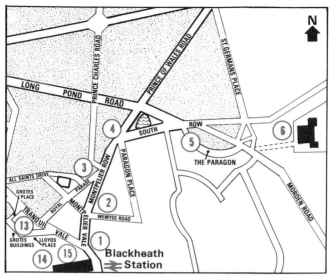

It has witnessed many historic events. Wat Tyler's rebels assembled here in 1381, prior to their march on London. The triumphant Henry V was received on the heath by rejoicing Londoners in 1415, following the battle of Agincourt. Jack Cade's revolutionaries met on the heath in 1450. Henry VII fought the Cornish rebels here in 1497 and it was at Blackheath that his son, Henry VIII, first met the plain Anne of Cleves who was to become his fourth wife. Inspired by Holbein's flattering portrait of 'the mare of Flanders', the King had agreed to marry her before seeing her.

Golf was introduced from Scotland by James I and the game was initially played in England on the heath. The Royal Blackheath Golf Club was the first to be formed in England and its members played here from 1608 until their amalgamation with Eltham in 1932.

It is uncertain how Blackheath gained its name. There are three possible sources: victims of the medieval Black Death were buried here; many robberies took place on the heath until the 19C; black gorse covered the area until it was burnt to amuse George IV's consort, Caroline of Brunswick.

Hollows in the heath, some of which now form ponds, were made for the excavation of gravel which was permitted until 1866. Others were filled with rubble from buildings destroyed during the bombing of London in the Second World War.

*• Continue ahead along South Row.*

| Location 4 | **SOUTH ROW** |

**Colonnade House** was rebuilt in 1804, possibly by *Searles.*

*• Continue ahead. First R Pond Rd.*

The entrance to **Paragon House**, *Searles* 1794, from
Pond Road has been embellished by the present
doorway, which came from the Adelphi, the late-
18C riverside development by the *Adam* brothers in
central London, below Strand.

*●* *Continue ahead to The Paragon.*

| Location 5 | **THE PARAGON** *Searles 1794–1807* |

This crescent is judged one of the finest in the
London area. Part of the colonnade is believed to
have come from a Palladian villa built on the site
early in the 18C by *James* for Sir Gregory Page. The
houses were damaged by bombs during the Second
World War but restored and converted into flats in
1951.

*●* *At the east end of The Paragon R Morden Rd.*

Some Regency houses survive in Morden Road.

Gounod, the composer, lived at **No 15** in 1870.

*●* *Cross the road immediately to Morden College.
Enter the gate and follow the path ahead.*

| Location 6 | **MORDEN COLLEGE** *Wren (?) 1695* |

*Open by appointment
only. Admission free.
(If no appointment has
been made the grounds
may generally be
entered to afford a
closer view of the
exterior of the
building.)*

Sir John Morden, a merchant who shipped goods to
and from Turkey, commissioned the college to
provide almshouses for 'decayed Turkey
merchants'. They now accommodate pensioners.

Above the entrance porch are statues of the founder
and his wife, probably added some time after the
building was completed.

The windows are original and represent one of
London's earliest examples of the sash method of
opening.

*●* *Pass through the central doorway to the
cloistered quadrangle and await the guide.*

In the centre of the courtyard are the remains of two
wells and an unusual lamp standard.

Each doorway from the cloister leads to individual
dwellings.

The chapel door faces the courtyard's entrance.

*●* *Enter the* **chapel** *with the guide.*

The carved reredos is allegedly by *Gibbons*.

Small stained glass figures in the east window were
made *c*.1600.

Morden, the founder, is buried within the chapel.

*●* *Exit from Morden College and cross Morden Rd
to the heath. Continue to the north side of the road
which lies immediately opposite The Paragon.
Proceed diagonally north-westward across the heath
towards the white painted block of two semi-detached
houses on the extreme west side. When these are
reached, cross Wat Tyler Rd to Dartmouth Hill.*

*●* *Alternatively, if continuing at this point with the
Greenwich itinerary, R Wat Tyler Rd. First R
Shooters Hill. First L General Wolfe Rd. Continue
ahead and then proceed R to Ranger's House.*

| Location 7 | **DARTMOUTH HILL** |
|---|---|

Immediately L the two white-painted, semi-detached Palladian-style properties, **Sherwell House** and **Lydia House**, were built in 1776.

**Nos 22** and **20** are late 18C. They originally formed one house which became the residence of the pioneer weather forecaster James Glaisher.

☛ *First L Dartmouth Row. Cross to the west side and continue southward.*

| Location 8 | **DARTMOUTH ROW** |
|---|---|

The name of this street commemorates an adviser to James II, Admiral Legge, later Lord Dartmouth, who purchased the entire Blackheath estate. He was granted a charter in 1683 for the Blackheath Fair, which is still held annually.

Dartmouth Row includes some of Blackheath's oldest properties which are passed as follows:

On the west side **Nos 20** and **22**, *c.*1700.

**No 28**, 1794.

**Nos 30** and **30A**, mid 18C.

**Nos 32–36A** mid to late 18C.

☛ *Cross to the east side.*

**Nos 21** and **23**, **Perceval House** and **Spencer House**, were built in 1689 as one property which was purchased by Prime Minister Spencer Perceval in 1812. Later that year he was shot by a bankrupt Liverpool broker whilst standing in the House of Commons lobby. Perceval is the only British prime minister to have been assassinated.

Above the windows are outstanding Coade stone figure keystones.

☛ *Enter the church next to Spencer House.*

| Location 9 | **CHURCH OF THE ASCENSION** |
|---|---|

The church was founded *c.*1695 as the Blackheath Chapel. Its nave was rebuilt in 1834 but the original 17C east apse survives.

☛ *Exit L and proceed to the adjoining house.*

| Location 10 | **DARTMOUTH HOUSE** *c.1750* |
|---|---|
| Dartmouth Row | |

The house was acquired for residential purposes in the late 19C by the College of Greyladies whose services were held in the adjoining church.

☛ *Continue ahead to St Austell Rd. First L Eliot Hill. Fifth R The Orchard. L Eliot Vale. First R Pagoda Gardens. Immediately R is Pagoda House.*

| Location 11 | **PAGODA HOUSE** |
|---|---|
| Pagoda Gardens | |

This residence, one of London's most bizarre, was probably built as a garden house for the fourth Earl of Cardigan *c.*1760.

It is believed that the upper, oriental features were added later for the Duke of Buccleuch *c.*1780.

The wing of the house was built in the early 19C.

•• *Return to Eliot Vale R.*

Passed R on the south side are **Eliot Vale House** and **No 9**. Both were built in 1805.

•• *Continue ahead to Eliot Place.*

| Location 12 | **ELIOT PLACE** |
|---|---|

Much of the street is composed of late-18C and early-19C properties which are passed as follows:

**No 1, Heathfield House**, 1795.

**Nos 4–5**, 1793.

**No 6**, 1797.

**Nos 7** and **8** are dated 1792.

**No 11, St German's House**, and **Nos 12** and **13** are early 19C.

•• *Continue ahead to the Hare and Billet pub. R Hare and Billet Rd. First R Grotes Place.*

Immediately R are **Nos 1** and **2 Grotes Place**. They are early 19C and two of Blackheath's prettiest cottages.

•• *The L fork in the road leads to Grotes Buildings R.*

| Location 13 | **GROTES BUILDINGS** |
|---|---|

These houses were developed 1766 by a German banker named Grote. The land is owned by Morden College, founded in 1695, hence the small wall plaque 'MC 1695'.

**No 2** was stuccoed early in the 19C.

•• *Continue ahead to Lloyds Place.*

| Location 14 | **LLOYDS PLACE** |
|---|---|

Immediately R is **No 4, Lindsey House**, 1774.

The last property, **Eastnor House**, is mid 18C.

•• *At the end of Lloyds Place follow the footpath R (Camden Row) which leads to Tranquil Vale.*

| Location 15 | **TRANQUIL VALE** |
|---|---|

At this north end of the thoroughfare, behind modern shop fronts, are 18C and early 19C houses, passed, on the west side, as follows:

Weather-boarded, next to The Crown pub, is **No 47**, 18C.

•• *First R* **Collins Square**.

**Nos 1–3** are picturesque mid-18C cottages.

•• *Return to Tranquil Vale R.*

**Nos 25–27** were built as Vale House in 1798.

**No 23** is mid 18C with a late Victorian shop front.

•• *Continue ahead to Blackheath Station (BR) and return to Charing Cross Station (BR).*

•• *Alternatively, if continuing to Charlton, take bus 54 northbound from the station to The Village, Charlton. From the bus stop return northward to St Luke's.*

# Charlton

Technically, Charlton forms a large part of the Borough of Greenwich, but only its ancient centre, 'the village', on top of the hill, is of particular interest to the visitor. Here can be found a rare Carolean church and, even rarer, a little altered Jacobean mansion, Charlton House.

*Timing*  Charlton House can be entered Monday–Friday and is best seen between 17.00–18.00 when few rooms are in use.

*Suggested connections*  Precede with Blackheath or Woolwich.

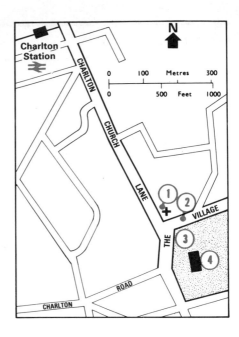

*Locations*
1 St Luke
2 The Village
3 Garden House
4 Charlton House

**Start** *Charlton Station (BR) from Charing Cross Station (BR). Exit from the station R Charlton Church Lane. Ascend the hill to The Village L (there is no bus service). Enter St Luke's churchyard.*

*Alternatively, continue from Blackheath or Woolwich as indicated.*

| Location 1 | **ST LUKE** c.*1630* |
|---|---|

Charlton Church Lane

St Luke's, constructed entirely of brick, is a rare London example of a church built in the reign of Charles I. Although still basically Gothic, some Renaissance features are apparent.

The manor of Charlton, named from a settlement of churls (free husbandmen), was given to Bishop Odo by William the Conqueror, his half-brother, in the 11C. Soon, however, it passed to the Priory of Bermondsey.

Charlton is mentioned in the Domesday Book and a Saxon church probably stood on the present site, although St Luke was first recorded in 1077. The present church was built with a legacy by Sir Adam Newton, who had purchased the manor from the Crown. Some of the fabric of the earlier walls was incorporated.

Above the first window of the nave is a sundial, a 1934 replica of the mid-17C original.

It is known that an earlier mid-15C legacy had led to some rebuilding of the chancel, and its existing south window may be a re-used survivor of this work. The chancel was extended in 1840.

The north aisle was added to the nave in 1639.

At the north-east corner of the church are vestries built in 1956.

The Dutch-style gabled porch is the only typically Carolean feature of the church. Its door is original.

●● *Enter the church from the south porch and turn L.*

The base of the **tower** serves as the baptistry. Its font is 17C.

Fixed to the roof, immediately above, is the sounding board of the 17C pulpit.

On the north wall of the tower is the large monument commemorating Grace, Viscountess of Ardmagh, d.1700.

The rounded arches of the **north aisle**'s arcade represent the most obvious Renaissance feature of St Luke.

Against the west wall of the aisle is the monument to Spencer Perceval. The bust is the work of *Chantrey*. Perceval, who is buried in the church, was the only British prime minister to be assassinated – in the House of Commons Lobby in 1812. (His house at Blackheath is described on page 25).

The north aisle's window includes 17C heraldic stained glass featuring the coats of arms of notable local families, including the Wilsons and Longhorns, owners of Charlton House.

A chapel was created in the north aisle in 1927. Its altar came from the chapel at Charlton House which had been consecrated and dedicated to St James in 1616.

The pulpit was made for the rebuilt church *c*.1630. It bears the arms of Sir David Cunningham.

On the south wall of the **south aisle**, just west of the chancel, is the monument to the Surveyor General of Ordnance to George I, Brigadier Michael Richards, d.1721 by *Guelfi* (?).

Past the door on the south wall is the wall plaque commemorating Edward Wilkinson, *d*.1567. He had been Master Cook to Elizabeth I and prior to this, Yeoman of the Mouth to Henry VIII, Anne Boleyn and Edward VI.

Near the entrance is the monument to Sir Adam and Lady Newton by *Stone*. Sir Adam, d.1629, was not only the benefactor who made possible the building of the present church, but also the builder of Charlton House.

●● *Exit from the church.*

In the **churchyard** is a flagpole from which the British Ensign is flown twice annually, on St George's and St Luke's days. The privilege was granted to the church to commemorate when, in the early 18C, the flag was flown from the top of the tower as a navigational aid to Thames shipping.

●● *From the churchyard, cross The Village immediately to the Bugle Horn inn.*

| Location 2 | **THE VILLAGE** |

Although little pre-dates the 19C, this quaintly named thoroughfare has preserved a village-like character.

The **Bugle Horn** inn retains some of its late-17C external appearance, but has mostly been rebuilt. Originally it was a two-storey cottage.

An internal staircase may be late 17C.

●● *Turn R and proceed westward. First L Charlton Rd. Immediately L are public toilets, once the garden house of Charlton House.*

| Location 3 | **GARDEN HOUSE** *Inigo Jones (?) c.1630* |

This is England's most important public toilet – from an architectural viewpoint. It was erected in the grounds of Charlton House, serving as a garden house. Later the building became an armoury and an estate agent's office. Many believe it to be one of the few surviving works of *Inigo Jones*, partly due to the uncharacteristically simple design for that period. However, *Nicolas Stone* has also been suggested.

The building's most notable feature is its rare example of a saddleback roof, rebuilt after Second World War bomb damage.

Its original doorway has been filled and the windows altered.

●● *Follow the road southward and proceed to Charlton House.*

In the grounds, facing the house, is a Classical archway built in the 17C but much altered. The front drive ran through this to the entrance.

| Location 4 | **CHARLTON HOUSE** *Thorpe (?) c.1612* |

Charlton Road
(856 3951)

*Open Monday–Friday. Best visited 17.00–18.00 when most rooms are unoccupied. Admission free.*

Charlton House is the least altered early-17C mansion in the London area. In 1923, following First World War use as a hospital, it was purchased by the local authority and now functions as a community centre. Although possessing no period furnishings, the house retains outstanding Jacobean woodwork, chimney-pieces and ceilings, some restored or remade as replicas. These features are preserved in reasonably good condition but appear rather incongruous amongst the general municipal drabness. Visitors must ponder on our cavalier treatment of such riches.

The manor of Charlton was acquired by Sir Adam Newton, Dean of Durham, after the dissolution of the monasteries. He demolished an existing manor house and commissioned the present building *c.*1612.

Charlton House originally overlooked the village green which was added to its grounds and enclosed in 1825.

The house was built in the usual H shape,

possibly by *John Thorpe*, the designer of Holland House at Kensington (mostly destroyed by Second World War bombing). The Wilson family owned the house from 1767 until 1915 and they made only minor changes to it, apart from restoration work (mostly by *Norman Shaw* in 1878).

Dominating the west façade is its exuberantly carved stone frontispiece. It has been recorded that this was reconstructed late in the 19C as a replica. The two coats of arms below the first floor window are 18C additions, those R being of Newton, the builder of Charlton, and those L of the Wilson family.

The north wing L with its tower was mostly rebuilt after war damage.

The south wing's tower is original but much restored. Its clock is dated 1784.

The bay on the south side has been rebuilt. Southern extensions were made in the late 18C, but the stable block is original, although somewhat altered.

All the Tudor style chimney-stacks are late 19C.

•➡ *Enter the house from the central door.*

It is possible to see most rooms, unguided, during an early evening visit. At other times, some may be occupied.

Most chimney-pieces and ceilings are 17C examples; many were installed by Sir William Ducie, a mid-17C owner.

The **hall**'s gallery was probably added early in the 18C.

The 17C-style panelling is apparently modern.

The ceiling and stained glass windows are reproductions of the originals.

Immediately L of the entrance is the **Jenkins Room**. This is fitted with a bar but was once the library. The original fireplace is intricately carved and dated 1612.

At the far end of the hall L is the entrance to the main stairway.

Ahead, the original doors of the **Wilson Room** and the **Chapel** are the best 17C examples in the house.

The richly carved **staircase** is original to the house and judged to be an outstanding example of Jacobean work. Decorative plasterwork around the stairwell was executed in the 19C.

Due to its height, the hall occupies much of the first floor and, in consequence, the most important rooms are unusually on the second and not the first floor.

•➡ *Ascend to the second floor.*

The **Long Gallery** lies L of the stairs. Its panelling is not original, apart from the pilasters on each side of both windows.

Stained glass incorporates the arms of the Ducie family and is a post-war copy of 17C work.

Adjoining the gallery is the **White Room.** Its chimney-piece has, in its central panel, a plaster copy of the original carving depicting Perseus and Pegasus. The frieze above illustrates the triumphs of Christ and of Death (on horseback).

The **Grand Salon** which follows, lies directly above the hall and covers the same area. Its much restored pendant ceiling is a rare example.

Windows again feature the Ducie arms.

Inscribed in the west bay is 'JR' the monogram of James I (Jacobus Rex).

The east bay features the Prince of Wales's feathers and motto 'Ich dien' (I serve). This almost certainly commemorates Prince Henry, eldest son of James I, who had been tutored by Adam Newton until two years before his untimely death in 1612, aged eighteen. John Evelyn, the diarist, was a friend of the Newton's and enigmatically recorded in 1652 that the house had been 'intended for Prince Henry's use'.

Figures flanking the marble fireplace represent Venus and Vulcan.

The chimney-piece in the **Dutch Room** that follows is made of black marble and its later Classical design, c.1660, contrasts with most of the others in the house that are earlier.

**Prince Henry's Room** has an outstanding carved fireplace.

•● *Exit from Charlton House R. Cross Charlton Rd and continue ahead to Charlton Church Lane and Charlton Station (BR).*

# Woolwich

For long one of London's most unjustly neglected areas, Woolwich is now becoming more widely appreciated by visitors following the completion of its Thames Barrier. At the same time, the historic Royal Arsenal buildings have at last been restored and can now be viewed by the public. The Royal Artillery Barracks presents a quarter-mile long unbroken Classical façade, the longest in England, and the regiment's Museum of Artillery is housed in a massive tent, designed by Nash early in the 19C to mark Napoleon's downfall.

*Timing* Monday to Friday is preferable, but if preceding with Eltham choose Thursday when Eltham Palace may be seen.

*Suggested connections* Precede with Eltham. Continue with Charlton.

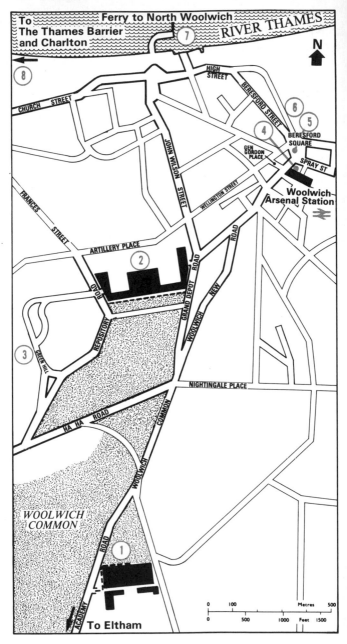

*Locations*

1 Royal Artillery Museum
2 Royal Artillery Barracks
3 The Rotunda
4 Simple Simon
5 Beresford Square
6 Old Royal Arsenal
7 Woolwich Ferry
8 Thames Barrier

**Start** *Woolwich Arsenal Station (BR) from Charing Cross Station (BR).
Exit L. If viewing the Royal Artillery Museum (Location 1) take bus 122 or
161 southbound to Academy Rd (request stop). Enter the main gate. Follow
the first drive L to the end. Proceed R through the car park.*

*Alternatively, if not viewing the museum, alight earlier from bus 122 or 161
at Grand Depot Rd. Cross the road to the Royal Artillery Barracks
(Location 2).*

*Alternatively, continue from Eltham as indicated.*

| Location 1 | **ROYAL ARTILLERY MUSEUM** *J. Wyatt 1808* |
|---|---|

Academy Road
(856 5533)

*Open Monday–
Friday 10.00–12.30
and 14.00–16.00.
Admission free.*

The block accommodating the museum stands on
the north side of the complex and overlooks
Woolwich Common. It was built to house the
Royal Military Academy which amalgamated
with Sandhurst in 1964.

The chapel was added in 1902.

Much of the remainder, including the end
pavilions, is late 19C.

The museum building has four corner turrets
topped with cupolas in imitation of the White
Tower at the Tower of London.

*•● Enter from the north side (past the library
entrance).*

Exhibits relate to the history of the regiment
since its foundation in 1716. Uniforms, badges,
tableaux and photographs are displayed in three
large rooms.

*•● Exit from the museum, return to Academy Rd
and cross the road. Take bus 122 or 161 to Grand
Depot Rd. Return southward, enter the grounds of
the Royal Artillery Barracks through the gate R.*

| Location 2 | **ROYAL ARTILLERY BARRACKS** |
|---|---|

Grand Depot Road .

*The grounds only may
be entered. Admission
free.*

Ahead, the longest Classical façade in England
stretches for approximately a quarter of a mile
and, as Pevsner suggests, invites comparison with
the palaces of Leningrad. It was mostly built
1775–82, by an unknown staff architect, but the
western section was completed to match by *J.
Wyatt* in 1802. The barracks can house 4000
troops.

*•● Cross the grounds passing the entire south
façade and exit at the west gate. L Repository Rd.
First R Green Hill. Continue ahead to The Rotunda.*

| Location 3 | **THE ROTUNDA (MUSEUM OF ARTILLERY)** |
|---|---|

Green Hill (off
Repository Road)
(856 5533)

*Open November–
April Monday–
Friday 12.00–16.00
Saturday–Sunday
13.00–16.00. May–
October open until
17.00. Admission
free.*

The Rotunda began its life as a canvas tent and
first stood in the garden of the Prince Regent's
Carlton House, now part of St James's Park. It
was one of six tents erected in 1814 to
accommodate meetings between sovereign heads
of state following the defeat of Napoleon. Their
erection was premature. The tent was presented
to the regiment by George IV in 1819 to house
their museum. Three years later, the structure
was made more permanent by *Nash*, who
covered it with lead and lined the inside with
timber. He raised the tent on to a brick wall,
adding columns and a central pillar for strength.

The sandwiched canvas and ropes remain but cannot be seen.

Guns and ammunition from all periods and many countries are displayed. The oldest gun exhibited was fired at the battle of Crécy in 1346.

*●● Return to the Royal Artillery Barracks and proceed eastward. Exit L Grand Depot Rd. First R John Wilson St leads to Woolwich New Rd. Continue ahead, passing General Gordon Place to Simple Simon's R.*

---

| Location 4 | **SIMPLE SIMON** |

5 Woolwich New Road

This restaurant is a rare survivor of the Victorian eel and pie shops that once abounded to the east of London, specifically to serve the poor. Its speciality is stewed eels, served with a 'liquor', a pale green sauce to which vinegar is usually added. Until 1985 this establishment was called the Pie Mash and Eel shop and retained its Victorian décor, including outstanding tiling. It has now, sadly, been modernized and the atmosphere lost. However, the eels remain.

*●● Exit R. L Beresford Square.*

---

| Location 5 | **BERESFORD SQUARE** |

*The market operates Monday–Saturday 09.00–17.00 but closes Thursday at 14.00.*

A lively streeet market helps to give Woolwich the atmosphere of a separate town rather than a London suburb. In 1987 much of the square is undergoing major redevelopment, particularly the old Royal Arsenal buildings on its north side.

*●● Proceed to the north side of the square and the gatehouse of the old Royal Arsenal (now isolated).*

---

| Location 6 | **OLD ROYAL ARSENAL** |

Beresford Square
*Opening details undecided.*

Although the manufacture of armaments here ended in 1967, the public were not permitted to view the outstanding period buildings that stood within the grounds and it was feared that none would be preserved. However, restoration of the most outstanding was completed in 1986. It is believed that some of the buildings were the work of *Vanbrugh*, whose Castle Howard was the setting for the television adaptation of *Brideshead Revisited*. No other examples of Vanbrugh's English Baroque work are known to survive elsewhere in the London area.

The gatehouse, built in 1829, was remodelled and an upper section added in 1897. This is now cut off from the rest of the complex by a new highway.

*●● Cross the road to the wall ahead.*

Behind the new wall lie the other Royal Arsenal Buildings that have survived.

The Royal Arsenal was founded as a military store in the 16C and was known as Woolwich Warre. It was situated near the Woolwich boatyard where Henry VIII's *Great Harry* had been built in 1512 and Charles I's *Royal*

*Sovereign* in 1637. It closed in 1869.

A royal laboratory opened here in 1695 and two pavilions were built. Following an explosion at Moorfields, it was decided in 1717 to transfer the Royal Arsenal to Woolwich as this was sited further from the capital and less damage would be caused by any similar accidents.

A brass foundry, together with a gun-boring factory and smithy which formed the entrance range to Dial Square, was built between *c.*1717 and 1720; these are the buildings attributed to *Vanbrugh*. Further ranges were added in the 18C and early 19C.

Immediately L is the **Old Brass Foundry**. Behind lies the **Guard House**.

**Verbruggen House**, *c.*1723, lies R and was built for the First Master of the Armouries.

Behind is a remnant of **Dial Square**. All post-mid-19C buildings have now been demolished.

'Royal' was added to the name of the Arsenal following a visit by George III in 1805. During the First World War, 75,000 were employed on the 1200-acre site.

The famous Association Football Club, Arsenal, which now plays at Highbury, was founded at Woolwich in 1886. The club was first called Dial Square as it was in these buildings that most of the players worked. Some had played for Nottingham Forest, whose scarlet colours they adopted. The team first played on Woolwich Common and soon changed its name to Woolwich Arsenal. In 1913 it transferred to Highbury and became simply, Arsenal.

*➡ Proceed to Beresford St, approached from the north-west side of Beresford Square. Take bus 177 or 180 westward to the Thames Barrier. Ask for Eastmoor St (request stop). Seen shortly R, from the upper floor of the bus, is the Woolwich Ferry.*

| Location 7 | **WOOLWICH FERRY** |
| --- | --- |

This pedestrian and vehicle ferry is a curiosity because it is the only completely free ferry in the world and will remain so, in perpetuity, by Act of Parliament. Ferry boats cross the river to North Woolwich, where the King George V and Royal Albert docks, in operation until only recently, now form part of the dockland redevelopment scheme.

*➡ From the bus stop return eastward. First L Eastmoor St. Proceed ahead to the Thames Barrier.*

| Location 8 | **THAMES BARRIER** |
| --- | --- |

*Riverside Walkway and Visitors Centre open. Admission free. Round the Barrier Cruises 11.00–16.30.*

This barrier was completed in 1982 to protect low lying parts of London from abnormally high water levels. Its piers have been likened to a succession of mini Sydney opera houses. The barrier itself cannot be seen, except during operational tests, or in the event of a flood warning, when it is raised in sections from the

*Also Woolwich to Westminster Pier Cruises.*

river bed. A riverside path provides a good view, but a 'Round the Barrier Cruise', lasting thirty minutes, approaches more closely. These depart from the pier, as does the boat to Westminster Pier.

An exhibition of how and why the barrier was constructed is housed in the Thames Barrier Visitors Centre. There are two film shows.

*● Return by boat from the pier to Westminster Pier.*

*● Alternatively, take the limited-stop bus to the centre of London.*

*● Alternatively, return eastward by bus 177 or 180 to Beresford Rd, Woolwich, and proceed to Woolwich Arsenal Station (BR).*

*● Alternatively, if continuing to Charlton, take bus 177 or 180 westbound to Charlton Church Lane. Ascend the hill to Charlton Village.*

# Eltham

The moated, royal palace of Eltham, with its hammerbeamed Great Hall, is a unique London survivor from the Plantagenet period. Eltham Lodge, a Restoration mansion, was designed by Charles II's architect, Hugh May, and is his only known work to remain in its original form. The Tudor 'Barn', and Elizabethan bridge that crosses its moat, are remnants from the estate of Well Hall, the home of Sir Thomas More's daughter, Margaret Roper.

*Timing*  Sunday or Thursday are preferable as only then can Eltham Palace be visited. Eltham may be thoroughly explored in half a day.

*Suggested connections*  Continue to Woolwich.

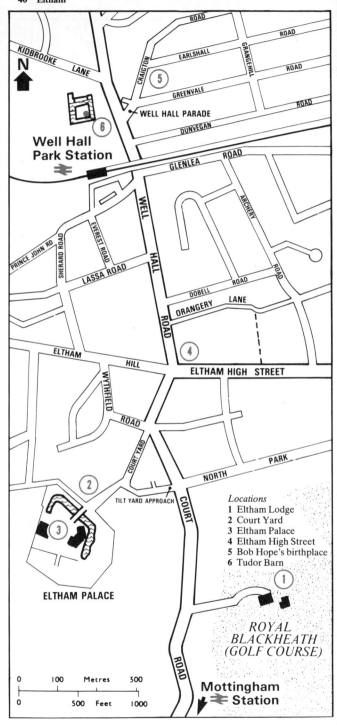

*Locations*
1 Eltham Lodge
2 Court Yard
3 Eltham Palace
4 Eltham High Street
5 Bob Hope's birthplace
6 Tudor Barn

**Start** *Mottingham Station (BR) from Charing Cross Station (BR). Exit from the station L. First L cross the railway bridge to Court Road. Continue ahead and cross to the east side of Court Road at the entrance to the Royal Blackheath Golf Club. Follow the short drive to the club house.*

| Location 1 | **ELTHAM LODGE (ROYAL BLACKHEATH GOLF CLUB)** *May 1664* |

Court Road
(850 1795)

*Open by appointment only. Admission free.*

*The north façade may be viewed at any time.*

Eltham Lodge was built, at the Restoration, for banker Sir John Shaw in the Dutch style on Crown Land. Shaw had acquired the entire Eltham estate in 1663 but assigned the surviving buildings of Eltham Palace to agricultural use. The lodge remained a private residence until 1880. It became the clubhouse of Eltham Golf Club in 1891. (The club merged with Blackheath Golf Club in 1932.)

*Enter from the north front and await the guide.*

Columns screening the **Staircase Hall** from the entrance hall were a later addition. The banisters are sumptuously carved with cherubs and foliage but have unfortunately been painted.

The **Morning Room,** L of the entrance, has rococo plasterwork framing portraits of Roman emperors.

Visitors are shown the first floor **Dining Room** when convenient. The ceiling and chimney-piece are original.

*Exit and return to Court Rd R. First L Tilt Yard Approach.*

The brick wall L, with its arch at the far end, originally enclosed the Tudor tiltyard where knights jousted.

*Continue ahead. L Court Yard.*

| Location 2 | **COURT YARD** |

This street originally formed one side of Green Court that stood outside Eltham Palace.

The first house seen R, **No 32**, is timber-framed but was re-fronted in the 18C.

**Nos 34–38** are half-timbered and were built in the 16C as the Lord Chancellor's Lodgings. Wolsey resided here as Lord Chancellor when visiting Henry VIII at Eltham. The buildings were remodelled in the 18C.

*Continue to the entrance to Eltham Palace. Immediately ahead lies the bridge.*

| Location 3 | **ELTHAM PALACE** |

Court Yard
(859 2112)

*Open Thursday and Sunday 11.00–17.00. Closes 19.00 April–September., Admission free.*

Eltham's royal connections go back to the 11C, when Bishop Odo, half-brother of William the Conqueror, acquired the manor house. A moated house was built on the site for Bishop Bek of Durham in 1296, and in 1305 he presented the estate to the Prince of Wales, later Edward II. Both Edward III and Richard II occupied the castle but only fragments of this building remain. Richard II's Clerk of Works at Eltham was

. Geoffrey Chaucer. It has been alleged that Edward III founded the Order of the Garter here.

Eltham Palace was largely rebuilt for Edward IV in 1480, with a new Great Hall as its centrepiece. It was then known as Eltham Court and remained popular with successive monarchs until the early part of Henry VIII's reign. After this, the palace was only used as a hunting lodge. Greenwich Palace, situated more attractively on the river, was preferred by Henry VIII, who rarely came to Eltham after 1529. The last sovereign to visit the palace was Charles I and he is only known to have come once.

At its height, Eltham was a large complex of many buildings grouped around courtyards but during the Commonwealth, it was sold by Parliament to Colonel Rich who demolished most of it *c*.1650. Sir John Shaw became the new tenant in 1663 but lived nearby, in Eltham Lodge, which he had commissioned to be built in the fashionable new Dutch style. The palace then functioned merely as a farm. The Great Hall, moat and bridge have been restored and the foundations of the chapel and royal apartments excavated.

Eltham Palace is now used by the army for educational purposes, although the Crown retains the freehold.

**Bridge.** This was probably rebuilt at the same time as the hall and much of the late-15C masonry survives.

**Moat.** The walls were first built *c*.1300 but replaced by the present moat walls for Edward III in the 14C and subsequently much altered and rebuilt, mainly in brick. Some of the lower sections of the inner walls, are, however, *c*.1300. Ahead, L of the bridge, the window in the wall was originally a sewage outlet. Flanking this are a 19C lion and unicorn by *Pugin* which were brought from the Houses of Parliament in 1936. Originally, the moat's water level was much higher.

At the end of the bridge L is a low brick structure, the remains of a **gatehouse**.

*⊷ Proceed ahead.*

Immediately L, linked to the Great Hall, is the house built for Sir Stephen Courtauld, who leased the estate in 1936. Standing behind and above can be seen timber gables of the lodgings *c*.1500.

*⊷ Proceed to the north façade of the Great Hall.*

**Great Hall.** This, the focal point of Edward IV's new palace, was completed *c*.1479 by master mason *Thomas Jordan*. During Sir James Shaw's 17C ownership the building functioned as a barn and continued to do so until it was partially restored *c*.1830.

The roof was rebuilt and most of the external stone facing above window sill level renewed *c*.1914.

The window tracery and the grotesque heads at parapet level have been restored.

The southern part of the palace grounds is not open to the public but the hall's façade on that side is similar.

*❧ Enter the hall.*

The hammerbeam roof was designed by *Edward Graveley*. Westminster Hall and the Great Hall of Hampton Court are the only larger buildings known to have been built with this type of structure. Eltham's hall possesses the earliest known example of hammerbeams with pendants (renewed *c.*1936 when the roof was restored).

The east gallery L was constructed from the screen *c.*1936.

Windows on the north and south walls are placed high to allow for the then fashionable display of tapestries beneath them.

*❧ Proceed to the west end.*

The dais and reredos were made *c.*1936.

To the north and south are bay windows. The design of their fan vaults incorporates Edward IV's emblem – a falcon and fetterlock. Originally, their bosses were of stone but these were replaced by plaster replicas *c.*1936.

*❧ Exit from the hall.*

The hall formed the south side of Great Court. To the west, running north and south of the Great Hall, were the Royal Apartments. Part of this range formed the west side of Great Court.

Immediately ahead, running parallel with the Great Hall, stood the Chapel which provided the north range of Great Court.

*❧ Turn L and proceed northward following the excavated foundations of the Royal Apartments.*

**Royal Apartments.** Excavations in the 1930s revealed the footings of this three-storey building that overlooked the Great Court. Outlines of bay windows, added for Henry VII in the late 15C, can be seen. The king's private apartments lay south of the chapel, whilst the queen's lay immediately to the north.

*❧ Turn R and proceed towards the moat bridge. Parallel with the Great Hall stood the Chapel.*

**Chapel.** Excavations were made in 1977 revealing extensive remains which have now been covered again.

Henry VIII rebuilt an existing chapel *c.*1515, and it was in this building that he appointed Wolsey Lord Chancellor of England in 1518. Two polygonal turrets at the west end led to the private apartments of the king and the queen.

*❧ Exit from Eltham Palace grounds. Ahead Court Yard. Continue to Court Rd L. First R Eltham High St. Immediately R is The Greyhound inn.*

| Location 4 | **ELTHAM HIGH STREET** |
|---|---|

**The Greyhound** is a 17C inn with, in its front bar R, a carved mid-16C stone fireplace, reputed to have come from Eltham Palace.

There is an attractive rear patio.

Next to the inn is **No 90**, **Mellins Wine Bar**, *c*.1700, with a later bow front.

*•➤ Cross to the north side and continue eastward.*

**Nos 97–100**, **Clifden House**, early 18C, originally formed one residence.

*•➤ Follow the path, first L, to the rear of the car park and the remains of an orangery.*

The early-18C brick-built **orangery**, with stone detailing is to be restored. It is all that remains from the Eltham House estate. Originally the Baroque building had a high centrepiece and a parapet.

*•➤ Turn L and follow Orangery Lane westward. R Well Hall Rd. Continue ahead beneath the railway bridge.*

*•➤ If viewing Bob Hope's birthplace: second R Well Hall Parade. Ahead, Craigton Rd. Continue to No 44 on the south side.*

*•➤ Alternatively, continue to the Tudor Barn, location 6.*

| Location 5 | **BOB HOPES'S BIRTHPLACE** |
|---|---|

No 44 Craigton Road

Here was born, on 29 May 1903, Leslie Townes Hope, now better known as Bob Hope. The infant lived here for three years before his parents moved to Bristol. One year later the family emigrated to Cleveland, Ohio, where their son later achieved fame and fortune as one of the country's most popular comedians. Bob Hope has since made return visits to Eltham.

*•➤ Return to Well Hall Rd R. Cross the road and continue ahead to the Tudor Barn (its grounds are entered L, immediately after the public toilets).*

| Location 6 | **TUDOR BARN (WELL HALL PLESAUNCE)** |
|---|---|

Well Hall Road

*Open daily 10.30–16.00. (Upper floor closed Saturday and some lunchtimes for private functions.) Admission free.*

A mansion named Well Hall is recorded as early as the 11C. The property was inhabited in 1524 by William Roper, husband of Sir Thomas More's only daughter, Margaret. Following her father's execution, Margaret Roper allegedly retrieved his head from Old London Bridge where it had been displayed on a pike, and kept it at Well Hall. More's head is now buried in the Roper Chapel at St Dunstan's, Canterbury.

The mansion itself was demolished in 1733 but the present 'barn', moat and a bridge survive. These, together with part of the grounds, were acquired by the local authority in 1936.

There were originally two complete moats encircling the mansion. First seen L is the Elizabethan bridge that crosses the inner moat.

*•➤ Cross the wooden bridge R. The 'barn' lies L.*

The building was unlikely to have been used as a barn as its chimney-stack and fireplaces on both floors are original. A simple barn would have had no need of these.

At the east end, immediately ahead, are restored turrets. Beneath their corbels are William Roper's monogram.

*•• Proceed ahead to the north façade.*

Most windows have been restored. The blind ground floor windows were originally plastered and painted.

In the centre of the north façade, at first floor level, is the coat of arms of the Tattersall family, dated 1568. They had been earlier occupants and the date was almost certainly a later addition.

*•• Enter the building.*

The ground floor has been converted to a restaurant.

Above, the first floor room is used as an art gallery or hired for private functions. Its beams and stone Tudor fireplace have been restored.

*•• Return to Well Hall Road R. Proceed to Well Hall Park Station (BR) R and train to Charing Cross Station (BR).*

*•• Alternatively, if continuing to Woolwich, take bus 161 (request stop) to the Royal Artillery Museum, Academy Rd. (Also a request stop.)*

# The East End

Since the arrival of the Huguenots in the 17C, much of London's 'East End' has provided a haven for ethnic groups, each of which has moved on and been replaced, in turn, by others. All have left their mark on the area. Much of the East End has a rundown, even derelict, appearance, and its charms are for those with catholic tastes. By the end of the century, redevelopment of the old docklands will have completely changed the East End along most of its riverside. Highlights are the Sunday street markets, riverside pubs, three great Hawksmoor churches and two unusual museums.

*Timing* All the major street markets are in full swing on Sunday morning. The Bethnal Green Museum of Childhood closes Friday. The Whitechapel Art Gallery closes Saturday.

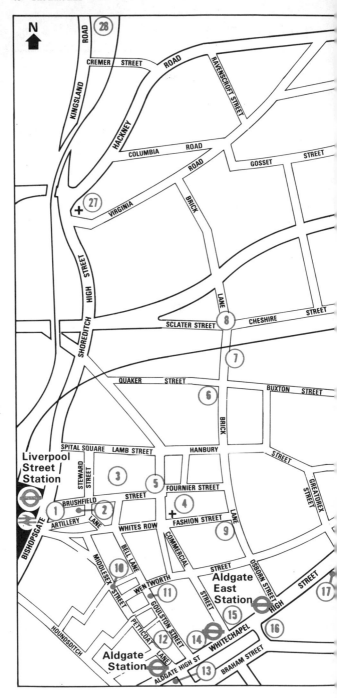

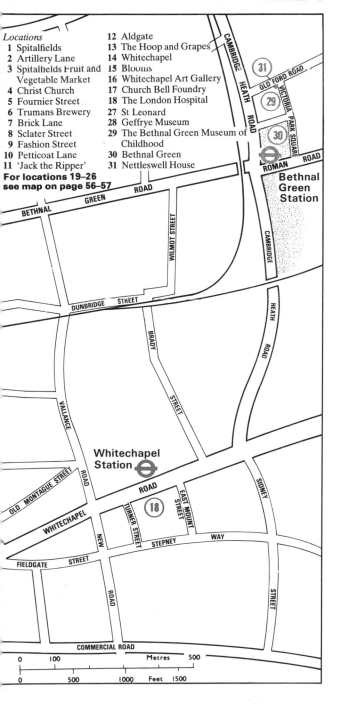

*Locations*

1 Spitalfields
2 Artillery Lane
3 Spitalfields Fruit and Vegetable Market
4 Christ Church
5 Fournier Street
6 Trumans Brewery
7 Brick Lane
8 Sclater Street
9 Fashion Street
10 Petticoat Lane
11 'Jack the Ripper'
**For locations 19–26 see map on page 56–57**

12 Aldgate
13 The Hoop and Grapes
14 Whitechapel
15 Blooms
16 Whitechapel Art Gallery
17 Church Bell Foundry
18 The London Hospital
27 St Leonard
28 Geffrye Museum
29 The Bethnal Green Museum of Childhood
30 Bethnal Green
31 Nettleswell House

Bethnal Green Station

Whitechapel Station

**Start**  *Liverpool Street Station (BR), Central, Circle and Metropolitan Lines. Leave the station by the Bishopsgate exit. L Bishopsgate. Third R Artillery Lane. Turn R at the Steward St junction and proceed to No 56A Artillery Lane ahead.  The area known as Spitalfields has now been entered.*

| Location 1 | **SPITALFIELDS** |
|---|---|
| | Many consider Spitalfields to be the heart of the East End. St Mary's Priory and Hospital at Lollesworth, the original name of Spitalfields, was founded in 1197. It was refounded as the hospital of St Mary Spital in 1235 and the surrounding meadows then became known as Spitalfields. The area remained basically agricultural until the French Huguenot silk weavers arrived in the 17C, bringing short-lived wealth to the area. Wages were low, however, and by 1807 the employees of the silk weavers were poverty-stricken. After 1825 the industry slowly dwindled but a few specialized weavers existed until shortly before the Second World War. Jews began to migrate to Spitalfields from Northern Europe *c.*1880 and spread rapidly to other parts of the East End. They, in their turn, have mostly been replaced by Asian immigrants. |
| | Henry VIII's Royal Artillery Company practised at Spitalfields in the 16C and street names such as 'Artillery' and 'Gun' commemorate this. |

| Location 2 | **ARTILLERY LANE** |
|---|---|
| | The shop front of No 56A, added to the house *c.*1757, is judged the finest mid-18C example in London. |
| | *Continue ahead. First L Crispin St. Proceed ahead to Bushfield St and cross the road to the market.* |

| Location 3 | **SPITALFIELDS FRUIT AND VEGETABLE MARKET** |
|---|---|
| Bushfield Street | Charles II founded this market by Charter in 1682. It was originally a street market, but houses were demolished to permit its extension to the present dimensions and the erection of market buildings in 1922. The fruit market is the largest in Britain. |
| *Market operates Monday–Friday, 06.00–1100; Saturday 0600–09.30.* | |
| | *Continue ahead to Commercial St and cross the road immediately to Christ Church.* |

| Location 4 | **CHRIST CHURCH** *Hawksmoor 1727* |
|---|---|
| Commercial Street (247 7202) | Christ Church, the largest of Hawksmoor's three East End churches, was built under the Fifty New Churches Act of 1711. The body of the church is reminiscent of the same architect's St Alfege at Greenwich. |
| *Open occasionally for concerts, otherwise apply at the crypt door L.* | Rebuilding of the spire in 1822 led to the disappearance of many of its decorative appendages. Other alterations to the church were made following damage by lightning in 1841. |
| | The windows, altered in 1866, have recently been restored to their original appearance. |
| | *Enter the church.* |

Because of dilapidation, and the restoration work being carried out, the church is only open on special occasions. It is intended that Christ Church will eventually match its original internal appearance with the restoration of north and south galleries and box pews.

The church retains its original font and lectern, together with a pulpit converted from the 18C reader's desk. These will be relocated in the church when building work is completed. Unfortunately, the reredos disappeared many years ago and its design is unknown.

Although Christ Church is virtually an empty shell, Hawksmoor's skilful handling of special elements is, as usual, immediately apparent.

The flat, coffered ceiling of 1729 has been restored.

On the north wall of the chancel is the monument to Sir Robert Ladbroke, Lord Mayor of London, by *Flaxman*.

Facing this, on the south wall, is the Edmund Peck monument by *Dunn*, 1737.

*Exit R. First R Fournier St.*

---

| Location 5 | **FOURNIER STREET** |
| --- | --- |

Fournier Street, built 1718–28 as Church Street, became a fashionable address for merchants and Huguenot silk weavers. Some of the houses, with their original carved doorways, are under restoration. Most retain their weaving attics with deep rear windows.

**No 2** was designed by *Hawksmoor* as the Christ Church rectory.

The large building at the end of the street L is a measure of the changing nature of the East End. Built as a church for French Protestants in 1743, it later became a Wesleyan chapel, then a synagogue, and is now a mosque serving the Asian community (**London Jamme Masjid**).

The sundial beneath the pediment is dated 1743.

•➡ *If it is Sunday continue ahead. L Brick Lane.*

•➡ *Alternatively, R Brick Lane. First R Fashion St (Location 9).*

---

| Location 6 | **TRUMANS BREWERY** |
| --- | --- |
| Brick Lane | A brewery has stood on the site since the 16C. |

Trumans buildings now combine 18C warehouses with a modern office block.

Horse-drawn drays have been reintroduced for local deliveries from the brewery.

---

| Location 7 | **BRICK LANE** |
| --- | --- |
| *Street market operates Sunday 09.00–14.00* | Although short, the Sunday street market in Brick Lane is one of London's liveliest. It begins with fruit and vegetables after the railway bridge and then becomes a general market. |

Indian shops and restaurants proliferate on either side.

In the 17C the lane was used by carts transporting bricks to Whitechapel from the nearby kilns.

At the Bethnal Green Road end, the Bagel Bakery sells bagels with various fillings – a Jewish speciality popular in the United States, though rare in London.

*➡ Return along Brick Lane. Second R Sclater St.*

| Location 8 | **SCLATER STREET** |
|---|---|

This extension of Brick Lane market has even more variety. At the far end, caged birds and animals have been sold for many years. Megaphone-wielding animal lovers are protesting against the conditions here and the trade is diminishing.

*➡ Return to Brick Lane and cross to Cheshire St ahead where the market continues. Return to Brick Lane L. Proceed to the railway bridge. Fifth R (after the bridge) Fashion St.*

| Location 9 | **FASHION STREET** |
|---|---|

A unique factory, known as the Fashion Street Arcade, occupies the south side. It was built as a bazaar and designed with Islamic features by *Abraham Davis* in 1905. This was prophetic, considering the later influx of Asian immigrants to the area. On a sunny day, a photographer could 'prove' he had returned from an area much further east than London's East End.

*➡ Cross Commercial St and proceed ahead to White's Row.*

**No 5** White's Row, L, is early 18C. Its original carved door surround survives, but the ground floor and basement windows have been altered.

*➡ Cross Crispin St. Ahead Artillery Lane. Where the road bends R continue ahead following Artillery Passage. L Sandys Row leads to Middlesex St.*

| Location 10 | **PETTICOAT LANE (MIDDLESEX STREET)** |
|---|---|

*Market operates daily but is extended on Sunday.*

The market in this street is less varied than it once was and tends to be dominated by new clothing. Most stallholders are still Jewish and many give an amusing 'spiel'.

The street was first recorded as Hog Lane, but the name Petticoat Lane was established by the 17C due to the Spitalfields silk industry. It was renamed Middlesex Street in 1832.

*➡ Third L Wentworth St. First R Goulston St.*

| Location 11 | **'JACK THE RIPPER'** |
|---|---|

Five prostitutes were brutally murdered in Whitechapel between 31 August and 9 November 1888. Their killer wrote to the police, signing himself 'Jack the Ripper'. The Whitechapel Murders were never solved and no one was ever charged. Many theories have been, and still are, confidently propounded. 'Suspects' have included Montague Druitt, Sir William Gull, Thomas Cream, Frank Miller, George Chapman, Sir Robert Anderson, Assistant Commissioner of

Police, painter Walter Sickert and the future Edward VII's eldest son, the Duke of Clarence. Also implicated have been Queen Victoria herself, Prime Minister Lord Salisbury and Sir Charles Warren, Commissioner of Police. Most of the victims lived in the streets of Spitalfields, around Christ Church, but their mutilated bodies were found between Aldgate and Whitechapel Road.

Apart from his letters, the only clues left by The Ripper were in a block of tenement flats that stood, until 1986, on the east side of Goulston Street, known as Goulston Street Buildings (later Wentworth Dwellings). An apron, stained with the blood of Catherine Eddowes, was placed at the foot of the stairs to Nos 118–119. Above it, on the wall, were the words 'The Juwes are the men who will not be blamed for nothing'. Surprisingly, Police Commissioner Warren ordered the immediate removal of the writing before it could be examined.

None of the streets where the bodies were found are of particular interest but some devoted 'Ripperologists' still like to seek them out. The victims, with the dates and locations of the murders, are as follows.

| Mary Nicholls 31/8 | Durrard Street (behind Whitechapel Station), then Bucks Row. |
| Annie Chapman 8/9 | 29 Hanbury Street, in the backyard. |
| Elizabeth Stride 30/9 | Henriques Street (off Commercial Road), then Duffield's Yard, Berner Street. |
| Catherine Eddowes 30/9 | Mitre Square (Aldgate). |
| Marie Jane Kelly 9/11 | Millers Court, Dorset Street; demolished for the Fruit and Wool Exchange. |

Some believe that the first victim was Martha Tabrum, alias Turner, whose body was discovered on 7 August 1888 on the first floor of George Yard Buildings off Whitechapel Road. As suddenly as they began, the Ripper murders ended. Their fascination for criminologists is as strong as ever.

*•* *Return to Wentworth St L. L Middlesex St. At the end cross Middlesex St by subway to the south side of Aldgate High St. Cross to the Hoop and Grapes opposite.*

| Location 12 | **ALDGATE** |

The name of the area is derived from an ancient gate, one of six that punctuated London's wall. First built by the Romans, it was named Ealdgate, i.e. old gate, by the Saxons. The gate was rebuilt in the 12C and Geoffrey Chaucer leased a room in it from 1374–85. It was again rebuilt in 1609 but, with the other city gates, dismantled in 1761. The structure was re-erected at Bethnal Green but only stood for a short time. Its original site was at the junction of Aldgate (the street) and Duke's Place. No trace of the gate survives.

| Location 13 | **THE HOOP AND GRAPES** |
|---|---|
| Aldgate High Street | This late-17C inn was dismantled and reconstructed in 1983 but, in spite of good intentions, little of interest survives internally. The legend of a tunnel leading directly to the Tower of London has not been confirmed. It is reputedly the oldest licensed house in London and was probably founded in the 12C.<br><br>●● *Exit and return to the west side of Middlesex St. L Whitechapel High St.* |

| Location 14 | **WHITECHAPEL** |
|---|---|
| | The parish of St Mary Whitechapel was established *c.*1338. Its name derives from a chapel built in the 13C. 'Nuisance' trades, such as metal working, were transferred here from the City in the 17C. When East European Jews migrated to the area 1880–1914 the second-hand clothing trade developed.<br><br>●● *Continue eastward passing Aldgate East Station's west entrance and proceed to Blooms restaurant.* |

| Location 15 | **BLOOMS** |
|---|---|
| 90 Whitechapel High Street (247 6001) | London's best known kosher restaurant was opened in Brick Lane in 1920 by Morris Bloom, who developed a new method of pickling salt beef. There is a take-away counter and a restaurant. Blooms is packed Sunday lunchtime, so arrive early if dining. It opens at 11.30.<br><br>●● *Exit L. Continue ahead towards Aldgate East Station's east entrance. The Whitechapel Art Gallery stands immediately before this.* |

| Location 16 | **WHITECHAPEL ART GALLERY**<br>*Townsend 1899* |
|---|---|
| Whitechapel High Street<br><br>*Open Sunday–Friday 11.00–17.50. Admission generally free but there is occasionally an entrance charge.* | The art gallery was specifically built to house avant-garde exhibitions. The Art Nouveau-style building, with arts and crafts reliefs, is reminiscent of Townsend's Horniman Museum at Forest Hill. Above the door is a mosaic 'The Sphere and Message of Art' by *Walter Crane*.<br><br>●● *Exit L and proceed to the public library immediately past the station entrance.*<br><br>On the wall L ceramic tiles illustrate a haymarket in the High Street in 1786. This market remained until 1927.<br><br>●● *Cross the road. Turn L and proceed eastward to the Fieldgate St junction (third R).* |

| Location 17 | **CHURCH BELL FOUNDRY** |
|---|---|
| 34 Whitechapel Road | This is the world's most famous bell foundry, probably established *c.*1420. Records go back to the 16C when the company moved from Houndsditch to Whitechapel; it transferred to the present site in 1738. The offices and shop were originally built in 1670 as the Artichoke Inn and its cellars survive. There was a coachyard at the rear which has now been taken up by the foundry. Big Ben and Philadelphia's Liberty Bell were both cast here. |

Inside the shop, above the door, is the original template of Big Ben.

*•● Exit R and continue ahead.*

Passed R is the **East London Mosque**, built in 1984.

| | |
|---|---|
| Location 18 | **THE LONDON HOSPITAL** |

Whitechapel Road

The hospital was founded in 1740 by John Harrison, a surgeon, and transferred here *c.*1751 when fields still remained in Whitechapel. Part of the original building, by *Mainwaring*, is incorporated in the present structure.

*•● Cross to Whitechapel Station, East London Line, and train to Wapping.*

*•● Alternatively, taxi to St George-in-the-East (Location 19), pausing to view its exterior, then continue in the taxi to the Prospect of Whitby (Location 21).*

The church exterior can also be seen later in the middle distance from Shadwell Basin.

| | |
|---|---|
| Location 19 | **ST GEORGE-IN-THE-EAST** *Hawksmoor 1726* |

Cannon Street Road

The church was bombed in the Second World War and only the exterior has been restored to its original appearance.

The tower is judged to be Hawksmoor's most distinctive.

Internally, the church is modern and dates from the 1964 restoration by *Bailey*.

*•● Continue by taxi to The Prospect of Whitby.*

*•● Alternatively, from Wapping Station exit R Wapping High St. First R Wapping Wall.*

| | |
|---|---|
| Location 20 | **WAPPING** |

Founded by the Saxons, initially on the north side of the river, Wapping derives its name from Waeppa's people. Wapping High Street was built up in the 16C but the area was essentially fields and market gardens until the London docks were formed in the 19C. Boat building and allied trades became established and later the warehouses, which still dominate the area, were built. It was at the Red Cow tavern in Wapping High Street that Judge Jeffrey, 'the hanging judge' was captured in 1688 attempting to escape to France. No trace of this building survives.

Oliver's Wharf, Wapping High Street, became, in 1973, the first warehouse to be converted into apartments. It marked the beginning of the extensive London dockyards redevelopment programme, due for completion by the turn of the century.

| | |
|---|---|
| Location 21 | **THE PROSPECT OF WHITBY** |

57 Wapping Wall

The inn was founded in 1520 but its present facade is Victorian. The famous waterside terrace has views eastward to St Anne, Limehouse.

Formerly known as the Devil's Tavern, the Prospect of Whitby gained its present name in 1777, as a ship from Whitby, ferrying coal from

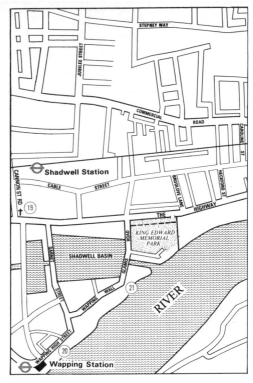

19 St George-in-the-East
20 Wapping
21 The Prospect of Whitby
22 Limehouse

23 Limehouse Basin
24 The Grapes
25 St Anne
26 St Dunstan

the North, was frequently moored outside the inn. This pub specializes in live entertainment and has a first floor restaurant.

The main bar has a low-beamed ceiling and the flag stone floor survives.

To the west, exact location uncertain, lay Execution Dock where condemned pirates were hanged and their bodies chained while three tides washed over them. Captain Kidd, the notorious 18C pirate, was executed there.

●● *Exit R. Wapping Wall. Continue ahead to Shadwell Basin.*

Canoeing facilities are provided free of charge on the basin.

The exterior of **St George-in-the-East** (Location 19) may be seen L with a backdrop of City skyscrapers.

●● *Proceed along Glamis Rd. R. King Edward Memorial Park. Enter and proceed through the park to The Highway. Passed R is* **Free Trade Wharf**, *an important part of the London*

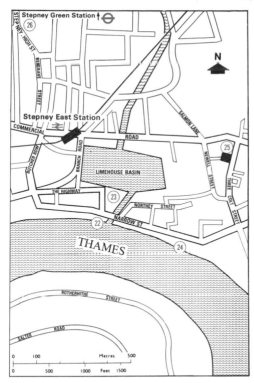

*dockyards redevelopment. Conversion to apartments and offices is underway. First R Narrow St. Limehouse has now been reached.*

| Location 22 | **LIMEHOUSE** |

The name of this area derives from the lime kilns which functioned in the 14C. Seamen resided here in the 16C and Limehouse later became a shipbuilding centre. London's first Chinatown was established around the Limehouse riverside when Chinese sailors began to settle *c.*1880. Although only about four hundred of them ever lived here, their gambling and opium smoking became notorious. Some Chinese restaurants remain, but following the Second World War, the Chinese population became centred around the southern section of Soho.

●● *Continue ahead to Limehouse Basin L.*

| Location 23 | **LIMEHOUSE BASIN** |

Here the Regent's Canal enters the Thames. The basin was created in the mid 19C but ceased operation in 1969. One quay is now reserved for pleasure craft. The docks R and the basin L provide picturesque views. North-east of the basin, the tower of St Anne's protrudes from a surprising number of trees.

●● *Continue along Narrow St.*

| Location 24 | **THE GRAPES** |
|---|---|

Narrow Street,
Limehouse

This Georgian riverside inn was featured by Charles Dickens in *Our Mutual Friend* as the Six Jolly Fellowship Porters. Unfortunately the river bar was 'Tudorized' in the 1960s. The first floor restaurant is open weekdays and gives good views; more important, however, is the riverside terrace.

*Exit R. Third L Three Colt St. L Commercial Rd.*

| Location 25 | **ST ANNE** *Hawksmoor 1724* |
|---|---|

Commercial Road

*Open for Sunday services only at 10.30 and 18.30*

St Anne's was consecrated in 1730, six years after completion. The reason for the delay is unknown. It was the first of Hawksmoor's three East End churches to be built.

St Anne's possesses London's highest church clock.

The interior, with its Greek cross plan, was influenced by Wren's St Anne and St Agnes but the nave is slightly longer.

The roof and most fittings, including the font and pulpit, were renewed by *John Morris* and *P.C. Hardwick* in 1857 following a major fire. Further restoration was carried out by *A. Blomfield* in 1891, and again after Second World War damage.

In the churchard is an unusual pyramid, the origin of which is unknown.

➠ *Exit L.*

West of the church is Newell St, formerly Church Row. Many 18C houses survive.

➠ *Turn R and continue to Commercial Rd. Take any westbound bus to Stepney East Station. Third R Belgrave St leads to St Dunstan's.*

| Location 26 | **ST DUNSTAN AND ALL SAINTS** |
|---|---|

Stepney High Street
(790 9961)

This is East London's most completely medieval church. Most detailing is 15C but within are features dating back to Saxon times.

It is believed that a small wooden church occupied the site until the late 10C when it was rebuilt of stone by Dunstan, Bishop of London. Initially, this church was only dedicated to All the Saints, but on Dunstan's canonization in 1029 his name was added. Rebuilding took place in the 13C and the chancel's structure survives from this period. The huge parish of Stepney covered all of Middlesex east of the City, until the 14C when the first of sixty-six new parishes were created in the area. Unless this subdivision had happened, St Dunstan's would undoubtedly have been rebuilt in a greatly enlarged form in the 18C. The aisled nave and tower were rebuilt in the 15C and it is the Perpendicular style of this period that therefore predominates. St Dunstan's parish once included Ratcliffe which, in medieval times, was London's port; the association between its church and mariners, therefore, became strong and many lie in its churchyard. Often referred to as the 'Church of the High Seas', births, marriages and deaths at sea were registered at St

Dunstan's until fairly recently. It is recorded that John Wesley preached here in 1785.

Externally, most of the building was refaced with Kentish ragstone in 1872.

In 1945 a flying bomb exploded in the churchyard and the resulting damage necessitated reconstruction of the upper part of the 15C **tower**.

The tower's west doorway was rebuilt in the 19C.

*Proceed clockwise around the church.*

Most detailing survives from the 15C but flint additions to the structure, and all the porches, are late 19C.

Some gargoyles survive but are much faded.

Although the fabric of the **chancel** is 13C its east window was rebuilt in the 19C.

On the south side there are traces of more gargoyles but the feature of greatest interest is the projecting **tower** that accommodated the stairs to the rood loft.

*Enter the church, generally from the south porch.*

The arcades on both sides are 15C.

Immediately L, against the wall of the **south aisle**, is the monument to Dame Rebecca Berry, d.1606.

Trusses of the aisle's 15C roof are supported by damaged figure corbels.

The **nave's** 15C roof also survives; its carved bosses have been gilded.

Above the west entrance are the arms of Queen Victoria.

Supporting the most westerly arch of the **north aisle** is a 15C figure corbel, partly concealed by the organ.

Behind the organ, on the north wall, is the early-17C memorial to Joseph Somes who, the epitaph relates, 'died of an unexpected internal malady'.

The font, in the north aisle, has been much remodelled, but its bowl probably has Saxon origins.

A 13C coffin lid is displayed at the east end of the aisle.

*Proceed to the centre of the* **nave**.

In the 15C the chancel was set back two bays and the arch removed. Its position is indicated by the cavity at upper level in the north wall where the rood screen, which stood beneath the arch, was originally fixed.

The roof structure also changes, where the arch stood.

Its first beam is decorated with 15C figure bosses but, unfortunately, most of the **chancel's** 15C roof was destroyed by a fire in 1901.

Above the chancel's north door is a 14C(?)

Annunciation carving which for many years stood outside the church.

On the north wall is a Jacobean monument to Robert Clarke, d.1610, and his daughter Frances, d.1620.

Below this is a squint which was discovered in 1899. It originally provided a view of the high altar but this has since been brought forward.

Further east, in a recess in the **sanctuary**, is the canopied tomb chest of Sir Henry Colet, d.1510. He was Lord Mayor of London in 1486 and 1495 and his tomb once provided an Easter Sepulchre.

On the east wall, behind the altar, is a stone 10C Saxon rood. Although it stood outside St Dunstan's until 1899, the figures of Christ, the Virgin Mary and St John may still be deciphered.

The mid-13C triple sedilia, in the south wall, retains carved foliage on its central arch and is the chancel's only original feature to survive.

Above the door is a memorial erected in 1621 to Sir Thomas Spert, d.1541. He had been Henry VIII's Comptroller of the Navy and founded Trinity House.

On the south wall is the entrance to the rood loft stairs.

West of this is displayed the stone from Carthage, with its grim inscription by Thomas Hughes, dated 1663. It appears to have been brought to England as a souvenir of a visit to the ancient site in Tunisia.

*● Exit R and continue to White Horse Lane. Cross Mile End Rd to Stepney Green Station, Metropolitan line. Underground to Liverpool Street Station, Metropolitan line. Exit R Bishopsgate. Bus 5, 6, 22, 22A, 35, 47, 48, 78, 149, 243A, 263A to Shoreditch church.*

| Location 27 | **ST LEONARD** *Dance the Elder 1740* |

Shoreditch High Street
(739 2063)

*Open Monday–Friday; 12.00–14.00.*

St Leonard's is one of three London churches designed by Dance the Elder, best known as the architect of The Mansion House. Apart from the usual Victorian removal of galleries and the lowering of the pulpit, little of this severely Classical but stately building has been altered. Its famous steeple remains an important East London landmark.

The first reference to the parish church of Shoreditch was made *c*.1145 when it was granted to the Priory of Holy Trinity at Aldgate, although, by tradition, there had been a Saxon foundation. Much rebuilding took place and by 1483 the medieval St Leonard's unusually possessed four aisles. In 1716 part of the tower collapsed and although the need for a new building had become obvious approval for this was not given until 1735. A strike by English builders protesting about the low pay rates accepted by Irish labourers working on the new church led to anti-Irish demonstrations. However, St Leonard's was completed within five years and became, in 1817, London's first church to be gas lit.

The west front is of Portland stone with the remainder of brick.

The **tower** follows the precedent set by *Gibbs* at St Martin-in-the-Fields, rising immediately behind the portico. Its 192ft high **steeple**, in spite of modern buildings, remains a landmark in Shoreditch.

The **north aisle** was rebuilt after the Second World War.

•• *Enter the church.*

It is immediately apparent that the interior is strongly influenced by the work of *Wren*.

Above the west doorway are the arms of George II.

The organ, in the west **gallery**, was made in 1756 and retains its original mahogany case.

On the front of the gallery is the clock which possesses an exceptionally fine carved surround attributed to *Chippendale*.

When built, the church also possessed north and south galleries but these were removed in 1857.

In the west corner of the **north aisle** is the font, made for the church from a solid block of marble in 1740. Further east, against the north wall, is a bread cupboard, unusually designed as a Doric temple. Its twin is fixed to the south wall, opposite.

James Burbage built the first English playhouse in 1576; it stood near the church and was called simply, The Theatre. The London Shakespeare League commemorated this by erecting a large monument against the north wall in 1903. Several Elizabethan players are referred to, including Gabriel Spencer who was mortally wounded by playwright Ben Johnson in a duel in 1598.

On the north and south walls of the **sanctuary**, boards record benefactors of the parish from 1585 to 1791.

The present east window's glass serves as a memorial to those who died in the Second World War. It replaced outstanding early-17C Flemish stained glass depicting 'The Last Supper' which had formed the east window of the previous church and been re-used. Unfortunately, this was not removed for safety in the Second World War and a bomb, which fell nearby, shattered it.

The altar was made for the church in 1740.

At the east end of the **south aisle**, against the wall, is the most dramatic monument in the church. This commemorates Elizabeth Benson 'in the 90th year the threads of her life were not spun to the full but snapped 17 December 1710'. The sculptor was *Bird* and he depicts the tree of life being snapped by two aggressive skeletons.

Further east, a simple plaque commemorates a parishioner, Dr James Parkinson, d.1824, who discovered the disease that bears his name.

The pulpit, which retains its canopy, was made for the church in 1740. It was reduced in height from a three-decker in 1857 at the same time as the north and south galleries were removed.

*←● Exit and proceed to the north side of the churchyard.*

Exhibited is the parish stocks/whipping post, protected by a roof which until recently, was thatched.

To the north-west of the church is 118 High Street, built in 1735 as the Clerk's House. It is believed to be the oldest private residence to survive in Shoreditch.

*←● Exit R. Cross Shoreditch High St. Bus 22, 22A, 48, 149, 243A to the Geffrye Museum.*

| Location 28 | **GEFFRYE MUSEUM** |
|---|---|

Kingsland Road (739 8368)

*Open Tuesday–Saturday 10.00–17.00. Sunday 14.00–17.00. Admission free.*

This museum of English décor and furniture opened in 1914, and covers the period from the Tudors to the 1930s.

The buildings were founded as almshouses for the Ironmongers Company with a bequest by a former Lord Mayor, Sir Robert Geffrye, in 1716. Originally, there were fourteen separate houses, each with its own front door; the central section was a chapel.

Shoreditch was an apt choice for the museum as it was, in the 18C, the centre of London's furniture industry.

*←● Exit L. Return by any bus to Liverpool Street Station then train to Bethnal Green Station, Central Line. Exit R Cambridge Heath Rd.*

*←● Alternatively, and again preferably, take a taxi direct.*

| Location 29 | **THE BETHNAL GREEN MUSEUM OF CHILDHOOD** |
|---|---|

Cambridge Heath Road (980 2415)

*Open Monday–Thursday and Saturday 10.00–18.00. Sunday 14.30–18.00. Admission free.*

The building's iron roof, by *Cubitt*, was originally erected as part of the South Kensington Museum, 'The Brompton Boiler', in 1856, on the site of the present Victoria and Albert Museum. It was re-erected here in 1872, encased externally with brickwork, and is now operated by the V & A as their doll and toy department. Exhibits include costumes, dolls' houses, toys, model theatres and puppets.

On the top floor, 19C continental furniture, sculpture and decorative art are displayed.

*←● Exit L. Cambridge Heath Rd. First L a footpath leads through Bethnal Green Gardens.*

| Location 30 | **BETHNAL GREEN** |
|---|---|

'Blida's corner' is believed to be the Saxon origin of Bethnal. Bethnal Green Gardens were the original village green. In the 18C weavers and dyers resided in the area which soon became the poorest in London. Furniture, shoe and clothing manufacturers later took over in Bethnal Green.

*←● Continue ahead to Victoria Park Square.*

**Nos 18–16**, immediately ahead, were built *c*.1700

*●▬ Proceed to the rear of the museum. Enter the courtyard and turn R to view Netteswell House.*

| | |
|---|---|
| Location 31 | **NETTESWELL HOUSE** *c.1660* |
| Old Ford Road | This is the oldest surviving property in Bethnal Green. Much restoration and alteration has taken place. The windows were changed from casement to sash in the mid 18C. |

*●▬ Return to Victoria Park Square L. First L Old Ford Rd.*

**Nos 21–15** are mid 18C.

*●▬ L Cambridge Heath Rd. Continue ahead to Bethnal Green Station, Central Line.*

# Ancient Churches of West Ham, East Ham and Barking

Most are astonished to discover that these three east London towns that once accommodated many dockers, although of relatively slight architectural interest, possess outstanding ancient churches. They are situated close to each other and may be easily visited on the same day. St Mary Magdalene, East Ham, is considered by many to be London's finest complete example of a Norman church. All Saints, West Ham and St Margaret, Barking, are basically late medieval with earlier elements.

## WEST HAM   ALL SAINTS

Church Street
(519 0955)

*Open Friday;*
*08.30–11.45.*

**From Central**
**London:** *Plaistow*
*Station, District and*
*Metropolitan lines.*
*Exit L. Take a*
*westbound bus to*
*Church St (West*
*Ham).*
**From East Ham, St**
**Mary Magdalene:**
*Bus S1 to West Ham*
*church.*

Although part of the core of 19C dockland, West
Ham possesses an ancient parish church which
has miraculously escaped rebuilding. It retains a
partially blocked clerestory and wall fabric from
the Norman period. However, most external
detailing is late medieval. Within, are a 15C tie-
beam roof, 13C arcades and some extravagant
17C monuments.

All Saints, founded in Saxon times, was rebuilt
c.1180. East and west extensions were made and
north and south aisles added to the nave c.1250.
The west tower was built and the nave extended
eastward c.1400. Aisles were added to both sides
of the chancel in the 16C.

The early-15C **tower** was completely restored in
1978. Its bell was made in 1857 as a prototype for
Big Ben.

•● *Proceed clockwise around the church.*

Partly blocked Romanesque clerestory windows
in the north wall of the **nave** indicate the length of
the Norman building.

The original stonework of the 13C **north aisle**
survives; at its east end the brick tower housed
the stairs to the rood loft.

In the early years of the Reformation, most
church plate was confiscated by the sovereign but
All Saints sold theirs just in time and built the
**chancel north aisle** of Tudor brick with the
proceeds. It was completed c.1550.

The east window of the **chancel** was rebuilt in the
19C.

It is believed that work on the **chancel's south**
**aisle** was begun towards the end of the 15C and
this, therefore, predates its northern counterpart.
Tudor brickwork survives.

The 13C **south aisle** was completely refaced in
yellow bricks in the 19C.

Again, on this side, the partly blocked Norman
clerestory survives in the **nave**.

The medieval '**Long Porch**' was reconstructed in
the 19C. A two-light, late medieval window, L of
its entrance, has been re-used from Stratford
Langthorne Abbey which owned All Saints' until
the Reformation.

•● *Enter the south aisle and turn L.*

Above the south-west vestry door, a lion and
unicorn flank the painted monogram of William
IV.

Both the nave's arcades were created in the mid
13C by piercing the Norman walls; they are
identical and possess circular piers.

The tie-beam roof was built throughout the nave
and chancel c.1500.

All Saints' possesses three fonts; its Victorian
example stands in the centre, at the west end of
the **nave**.

A west organ gallery was removed in the 19C and the arch to the base of the **tower** was thereby reopened.

Inserted in the north wall of the tower in 1903 was the stone decorated with skulls, which also came from Langthorne Abbey.

In the **north aisle**, at the west end, is a medieval font.

At the east end is another font, inscribed with the names of three churchwardens and the date 1707.

Fixed to the beam of the chancel arch are the arms of George II.

●● *Proceed to the* **chancel's north aisle**.

The piers of both the chancel's 16C aisles are octagonal.

With the removal of the west gallery in the 19C the organ was re-sited here.

The tie-beam roof of the chancel, *c.*1500, continues that of the nave.

Against the north side of the east wall of the **sanctuary** is the monument to Thomas Foot, Lord Mayor of London, d.1688, and his wife, Elizabeth. There is no family connection with Michael Foot, the ex-leader of the Labour Party.

On the same wall, in a pedimented niche to the south, is the monument to James Cooper, d.1724, and his wife.

*George Gilbert Scott* was responsible for the late-19C restoration of the church and the reredos was made to his design.

Against the south wall of the sanctuary are monuments to John Faldo, d.1613, and Francis, d.1632.

The chancel's south aisle was partitioned to form the **St Thomas Chapel** in 1966. Its name was chosen to commemorate an adjacent parish that had recently been integrated with West Ham.

Lettering, painted in the 16C, was discovered above the chapel's north arch in 1977 and this has been preserved by the Passmore Edwards Museum.

Against the chapel's north wall is the monument to William Fawcett, d.1631, his wife and her second husband.

A monument on the west wall by *Edward Stanton* commemorates several of the Buckeridge children who died between 1698 and 1710.

●● *Exit from the church*.

A school once stood in the churchyard where, in 1723, girls were given public education for the first time in England.

## EAST HAM   ST MARY MAGDALENE

High Street South
(470 0011)

**From Central
London:** *East Ham
Station. Bus 101 or S1
to Norman Rd.*
**From Barking, St
Margaret:** *Barking
Station to East Ham
Station; proceed as
above.*
**From West Ham, All
Saints:** *Bus S1 to
Norman Rd.
Both stations are on
the District and
Metropolitan lines.
The church is
approached from
Norman Road and
lies within the
Passmore Edwards
Nature Reserve.*

Standing in England's largest churchyard, now a
nature reserve, St Mary's is one of the finest
examples of a complete Norman church in the
London area. Original Romanesque features
include three windows, a well-preserved portal
and an apse which retains its unique, unrestored
timber roof, *c.*1130.

The body of the church was constructed *c.*1130.

The **west porch**, now serving as a vestry, was built
in the 19C.

•● *Proceed clockwise around the church.*

The **tower** was added early in the 13C but rebuilt
in the 16C. It is of stone with brick castellations.

The brick buttresses of the tower are 16C.

The round-headed first window on the north side
of the **nave** is typically Norman.

Two larger windows that follow replaced Norman
originals in 1845.

At the east end of the north wall of the **chancel** is
the doorway to what was a hermit's cell.

The east apse is a rare Norman example to
survive, most chancels were extended and
squared off in the 13C. Its buttresses were
constructed to support an internal vault.

On the south side of the chancel is a three-light
17C window.

The **nave**'s most easterly south window is 19C
and replaced a 14C example which had itself
replaced a Norman predecessor.

East of the restored south porch is the third
Norman window.

The most westerly window is, again, a 19C
replacement.

•● *The church must generally be viewed with a
guide from the Passmore Edwards Museum and
will probably be entered from the south porch.
Turn L.*

Between the nave and the tower is the
outstanding Norman **portal**. For a short time its
west side faced the elements but the construction
of the tower in the 13C, and its 16C replacement,
has helped to preserve the mouldings.

Internal buttresses to the tower, in both west
corners, were built in the 16C.

•● *Return eastward along the* **nave**.

Fixed to the pews on both sides of the nave's
central alley are churchwardens' prickers, dated
1805. Parishioners lulled to sleep by the long
sermons were awakened by a sharp jab.

The font, east of the south door, comprises a
bowl of 1639 on a late-17C stem.

A blocked section of a Norman window survives

adjacent to the nave's third window from the west on the south side.

Against the south wall, at the east end, is the alabaster monument to William Heigham, d.1620, and his wife; this originally stood in the apse.

Behind the lectern is a blocked door with, below, a holy water stoup.

*▸ Cross to the north wall of the* **chancel**.

Next to the pulpit is the staircase that once led to the rood loft.

Most of the chancel's north wall is blind-arcaded with a typical Norman interlaced design. This was repeated on the south wall opposite until mainly destroyed by the insertion of the 17C window.

The monument to Giles Breame, d.1621, is fixed to the north wall at upper level.

Below this is part of the early-16C opening to a hermit's cell.

Fixed to the arch of the apse is a Flemish painting of the Virgin, probably 16C.

Above the arch to the apse are traces of a medieval wall painting.

Fixed by wooden pegs, the unrestored Norman roof timbers, discovered in 1931, are a unique survival in England.

Evidence suggests that there was originally a stone vault which presumably collapsed at some time.

A large early-17C alabaster monument commemorates Edmund Nevill, Lord Mortimer, and his family. Nevill claimed a right to the earldom of Northumberland, hence the coronet on his wife's head, but this was disputed.

Immediately south of the east window is a pilaster which would have supported the stone vault. Evidently there is another example on the north side, now hidden by the Nevill tomb.

On the south wall is a 13C double piscina.

This is followed by a 13C priest's door.

*▸ Exit from the church.*

East Ham's churchyard of 9½ acres is reputedly the largest in England. It is now a nature reserve managed by the Passmore Edwards Museum.

## BARKING   ST MARGARET

London Road

*Open Thursday and
Friday 09.30–12.00.*

**From Central
London:** *Barking
Station. Exit R from
Barking Station and
continue ahead
following East Street
to London Road; the
church lies ahead.*
**From East Ham,
St Mary Magdalene:**
*Bus 101 or S1 to East
Ham Station;
Underground to
Barking Station;
proceed as above.*
**From Hornchurch,
St Andrew:**
*Upminster Bridge
Station to Barking
Station; proceed as
above.
All stations are on the
District and
Metropolitan lines.*

Barking's parish church retains its 13C chancel;
most of the remainder is late medieval.

St Margaret's was built within the precincts of
Barking Abbey, *c.*1216. It has always served the
parish and remained entirely separate from the
massive abbey church which was demolished at
the Reformation; this is why it escaped
destruction. The original chancel survives, but
most of the present building was constructed in
the 15C and 16C. Unusually, St Margaret's
possesses two north aisles. Captain Cook, the
explorer, married in this church.

Externally, St Margaret's offers a picturesque
scene. Its churchyard is approached through the
arch of the Curfew, or Fire Bell Tower, the only
structure remaining from the abbey; this is
described later.

Stone foundations of more abbey buildings were
found, north of the church, during excavations in
1910.

•● *Continue ahead to the tower of the church.*

The **tower** with its north stair turret, was built of
Reigate stone in the late 15C. Until 1894 the bells
were rung at 08.00 and 17.00 during the winter
months to guide travellers across the marshes in
the twilight.

Its doorway is modern.

•● *Proceed clockwise around the church.*

Stretching behind the stair turret is the **inner
north aisle.**

Attached to this is the gabled west end of the
**outer north aisle** which was added between 1501
and the mid 16C. Work began at the centre,
continued to this end, and was then completed
westward.

The early-16C **north porch** has two blocked
arches and its outer spandrels are decorated with
the Tudor rose.

Before the eastern part of the aisle's wall was
built the abbey was demolished and some of its
Norman stonework re-used here.

•● *Continue past the north-east door, now the
usual entrance, and proceed to the chancel.*

The **chancel** survives from the church of *c.*1216.
Lancet windows remain in the north and south
walls but its east window is early 16C.

South of the chancel is the 15C **vestry.**

The eastern section of the **south aisle**'s wall is
early 15C.

Brick buttresses have been added to support the
central section of the wall which began to lean
outwards; much of this part of the wall is early
13C.

Past the last buttress, the western section of wall
is late 15C.

*● Continue to the north-east doorway and enter the church. Turn R and proceed westward along the* **outer north aisle***.*

The arcade's octagonal piers are 16C.

The roof, which resembles a wooden boat, was probably built by local shipwrights.

At floor level, just past the porch, are the top sections of two windows (one partly hidden by a heater), indicating that the floor level here has been greatly raised.

Against the wall is the tomb of William Pownsett, d.1553.

West of this, a two-light window from the old abbey has been built into the wall.

Towards the most westerly window is the monument to Dr John Bamber, d.1753; the bust is believed to be by *Roubiliac*. It is protected by the original railings.

In the north-west corner, a monument commemorates Bamber's son-in-law, Crisp Gascoigne, who became, in 1753, the first Lord Mayor of London to reside at the Mansion House. The well known television presenter and author, Bamber Gascoigne, is a descendant.

*● Proceed to the* **inner north aisle***.*

Much of this aisle's arcade is early-13C work but its most westerly bay was rebuilt in the 15C with a higher arch.

The medieval timber roof was revealed in 1929 with the removal of the plaster; some repair and replacement was necessary.

*● Proceed to the area at the base of the* **tower***.*

Above the west door is a platform which is enclosed by the rail that once protected the high altar.

The royal arms are Hanoverian.

A shrine from Barking Abbey has been inserted within the tower's north-east pier. Standing in this is a glass case containing part of the shaft of a 7C Saxon cross.

The nave's roof had also been plastered but when this was removed in 1931 its woodwork was found to be in good condition.

The **south aisle**'s piers were renewed in the late 15C.

*● Proceed to the west end of the* **south aisle***, now the baptistry.*

The font, made *c*.1635, was removed in 1872 and its bowl and stem eventually became detached; they were reunited and returned to the church in 1928.

On the north wall is the monument to Sir Orlando Humphreys, d.1737; its rail is original.

The south arcade's most westerly bay, like the north arcade's, was entirely rebuilt in the 15C and, similarly, its arch is higher.

At the east end of the aisle's south wall, facing the pulpit, is a small recessed double arch. This was discovered in 1929, together with part of a newel staircase. Both are believed to have once formed part of the access to the rood loft.

A plaster ceiling at this end of the aisle was removed in 1929 to reveal the timber roof.

The aisle continues to form the Chapel of Youth, created when the organ was removed in 1929.

Figures on the altar screen include prison reformer Elizabeth Fry who is buried nearby in the Quaker cemetery and explorer Captain Cook who was married at St Margaret's in 1762.

•● *Proceed to the east end of the* **nave**.

St Margaret's once had a crossing and transepts which is why both the most easterly bays of the nave's arcades are wider.

The pulpit is 18C.

Above the chancel arch is a beam which retains traces of medieval painting.

The chancel's screen was made in 1891.

The vaulted roof of the **chancel** was plastered in 1772.

Both its arcades were renewed in the 15C.

On the north wall of the **sanctuary** is the monument to Francis Fuller, d.1636, possibly by *Stone*.

Below this, an incised stone slab commemorates Martinus, d.1328, the first recorded vicar of the church.

The recess with a brick moulding was once an Easter Sepulchre.

On the east wall, north of the altar, is an aumbry.

The piscina with its Norman shaft, on the south wall, was discovered in 1929.

Next to this, Sir Charles Montague, d.1626, is depicted on his monument as a cavalier in a battle tent.

The south lancet window, overlooking the altar, retains some medieval decoration.

Two Jacobean chairs stand in the sanctuary.

North of the chancel is the organ, originally sited in a gallery at the west end of the church. Its case was made in 1772.

West of the organ, a triple arch is built into the wall facing the inner north aisle; this probably came from Barking Abbey after its demolition in 1541.

•● *Proceed to the* **outer north-east chapel**.

The circular, Norman piers on the south side are also believed to have come from Barking Abbey.

On the north wall, beneath the window, a 12C

marble slab commemorates Mauritius, Bishop of London, 1085–1108 and Alfgiva, Abbess of Barking.

The window above was reconstructed from the original stonework, found nearby in 1928. It had previously been filled with the monument which has been re-sited west of it.

This monument commemorates Captain John Bennett, d.1706, and is decorated with outstanding carvings of nautical items.

A small, framed list of abbesses of Barking, R of Bennett's monument, includes Mary Becket (1173–5). She was a sister of Thomas à Becket, Archbishop of Canterbury, and no doubt her appointment by Henry II was due to the King's remorse following the archbishop's murder in his cathedral.

*Request permission to view the **Curfew Tower** and exit from the church with guide.*

Barking Abbey was founded as a Benedictine nunnery c.666 by St Erkenwald whose sister, St Ethelburga, became its first abbess. The abbey's 12C church was demolished along with the other monastic buildings in 1541. Only this, the Curfew (or Fire Bell) Tower, one of its three gateways, was reprieved. It was built in 1370 but reconstructed in 1460.

Before the tower of the parish church was built in the late 15C, a bell was rung from a small turret in this tower to summon parishioners to services. There is no record of either a curfew or a fire bell having been installed, in spite of the tower's name.

*Ascend the stone newel staircase to the first floor.*

This floor is dedicated as the **Chapel of the Holy Rood**. The mid-12C(?) stone rood is believed to have once stood outside the abbey walls as it appears to be weather-worn.

There are two blocked windows in the room.

Modern shields feature the arms of Barking Abbey, the Archbishop of Canterbury, the Bishop of Chelmsford and the old Borough of Barking.

# Docklands

London's five-thousand acres of redundant docklands have presented the capital with a unique opportunity to redevelop a vast area adjacent to its financial centre, and a new 'Metropolitan Water City of the twenty-first century' is rapidly emerging from the desolation. Completion is not expected until the early years of the next century, but progress is well ahead of schedule and the importance of this spectacular regeneration has suddenly become apparent with the opening of the Dockland Light Railway (DLR), which dramatically transports the visitor on 'stilts' from the City through the centre of the Isle of Dogs. Development on the riverside itself, between London Bridge and Greenwich, is best observed from the riverboats which operate throughout the year from central London.

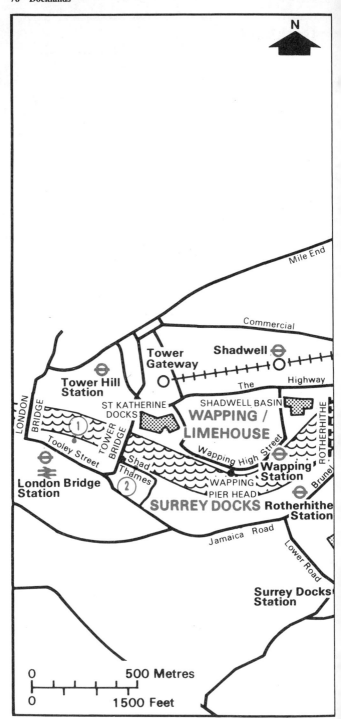

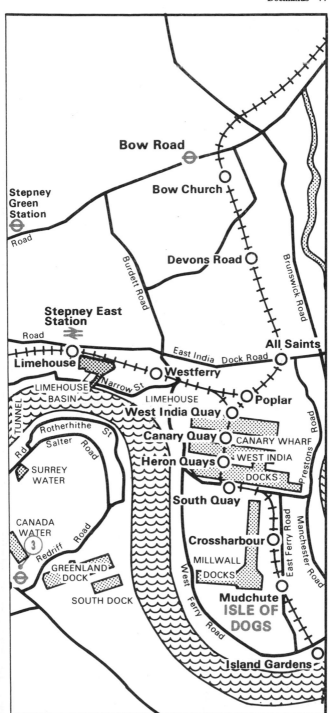

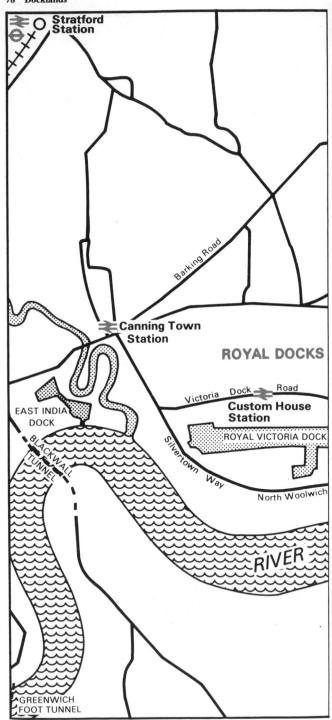

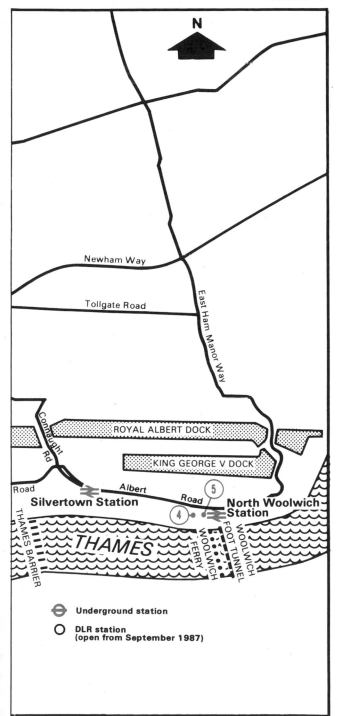

N

Newham Way

Tollgate Road

East Ham Manor Way

Connaught Rd

ROYAL ALBERT DOCK

KING GEORGE V DOCK

Road

Albert

Road

**Silvertown Station**

⑤

④

**North Woolwich Station**

THAMES

THAMES BARRIER

WOOLWICH FERRY

WOOLWICH FOOT TUNNEL

⊖ Underground station

○ DLR station
(open from September 1987)

### The Heritage

Throughout the nineteenth and much of the present century, London's docks have been among the most important in the world. However, modern cargo-handling techniques, particularly containerization, led to their demise between 1968 and 1981 and an enormous area of warehouses lining both the river Thames, and the docks connected to it, became redundant – together with a 24,000 work force.

In 1981 the London Docklands Development Corporation (LDDC) was created by the government to oversee the regeneration of 8½ miles of dockland. Unfortunately, in compliance with earlier policy, major docks in Wapping and Rotherhithe had already been filled, but extension of this work was immediately halted as the environmental importance of the inland 'lakes' became obvious.

The area north of the Thames from Tower Bridge to North Woolwich has been divided, for administrative purposes, into three zones: Wapping and Limehouse, Isle of Dogs and Royal Docks. South of the Thames from London Bridge to Rotherhithe and Downtown, lies one zone – Surrey Docks.

### An auspicious time

A combination of events has led to a speedier fulfilment of 'project Docklands' than even the optimists had dared to expect. The worldwide success of the City's financial service industries made its physical expansion outside the inhibiting and expensive 'square mile' imperative.

High technology of the 1980s, greatly indebted to the computer chip and space satellites, has meant the revitalization of old, and the creation of new industries, particularly in the field of communications. To take full advantage of these developments, completely new buildings, 'plugged in' to this modern technology, were required. Docklands was waiting to accommodate them on the City's doorstep.

An added encouragement was that by 1981 the environmental advantages of conserving and adapting ancient buildings of quality had become accepted and the new architectural style, Post-Modernism, combined sympathetically with them. At last it was apparent that ambitious schemes did not have to end up like the arid concrete jungles which had disfigured much of Britain throughout the three postwar decades.

### The scheme

The LDDC was given the authority to determine planning applications for Docklands although the area remained, for other purposes, within the jurisdiction of the relevant London boroughs. From the outset it was accepted that commercial and industrial premises should be situated side by side with housing, shopping centres and recreational facilities, rather than separated, as in the past. To encourage businessmen, much of the Isle of Dogs was designated London's first and only Enterprise Zone where, until 1992, no rates would be paid and capital investment could be offset against tax. From an early stage, a new airport, primarily for businessmen, was incorporated in the scheme.

### Achievement

Even before the LDDC was created it had become apparent that many of Dockland's warehouses, some of which were highly regarded architecturally, could be economically converted to other uses, primarily residential. The first scheme, on the riverside, had been completed in 1971 and one of the flats, originally priced at £12,000 was offered in the mid-1980s for £350,000, an indication of their popularity. Much of this early development of Docklands was, therefore, conversion work of this type, but with the completion of site preparation, services and access roads, new building work began and by 1987 practically all the available land in the Enterprise Zone had been taken and Docklands accommodated five national newspaper groups.

Rapid transport to the City was a prime requirement and in a short space of time Stage 1 of the Docklands Light Railway was built. The specially constructed track, raised on stilts 40ft above ground level, runs from Tower Gateway Station (open July 1987) which is a short walk from the existing Tower Hill Underground station, to Island Gardens station on the Isle of Dogs. A western extension to Bank station, in the heart of the City, is planned for the early 1990s and an eastward extension to Royal Docks is expected to follow.

New piers along the riverside have been built and a high-speed riverbus will operate from Chelsea to much of docklands, once the proving service, commencing summer 1987, has been assessed.

### Wapping

Due to its close proximity to the City and the accessible Underground stations at Tower Hill, Shadwell and Wapping, this section of Docklands has been the first to gain popular appeal. Unfortunately, its large Eastern and Western docks were filled and only a narrow canal indicates their previous existence. However, St Katharine Docks, Shadwell Basin and Limehouse Basin remain. In 1968 St Katharine Docks, created by Telford in 1827, became London's first to close, and its early and successful rehabilitation gave much of the impetus to the entire scheme. Telford's warehouses were either retained or rebuilt as replicas and now accommodate the World Trade Centre and the London Commodity Exchange. Housing, shops, restaurants and a pub were also incorporated. Newly built, between the river and the docks, is the Tower Hotel. The old docks themselves now serve as a boat marina.

Historic buildings further east include Wapping Pier Head, a Regency square, built in 1811 for Port of London officials, riverside pubs and two churches built by Hawksmoor. Much of this area is described in detail between pages 55 and 60, accompanied by a large-scale map.

### Isle of Dogs

This is, without doubt, Docklands' most important sector and, fortunately, its great West India and Millwall docks have not been filled in. It is best appreciated by travelling on the DLR to the terminus at Island Gardens. Spectacular water views are soon reached and progress at Canary Wharf may be observed. Located in the centre of the Enterprise Zone, the £1.5 billion Canary Wharf project is Docklands' most important. This virtually forms an extension of the City but will provide an international banking and finance centre in its own right. Practically all the available sites on the Isle of Dogs have been acquired and by the early 1990s an impressive modern city will have emerged. From the Island Gardens terminus, the famous 'Queen's View' of Greenwich, famous from picture books and calendars, may be observed. Greenwich centre can easily be reached from here, via the adjacent ¼-mile foot tunnel and a return to central London made from Greenwich Station or riverboat. (See pages 2–20).

### Royal Docks

This, the most water-filled sector of Docklands, will be the last to be completed, but the British Telecom Teleport is already functioning and, between the Royal Albert and George V docks, is London City Airport (open late 1987). This is a Short Take-Off and Landing airport (STOLPORT) and will facilitate business travel between London and British and North European cities within a 400-mile radius; no jets will be permitted due to strict noise and operating controls. Visitors will not see much at Royal Docks for some years and the simplest access will be via Stratford Station, Central line and BR to North Woolwich. Near the terminus lies the British Telecom Teleport and the North Woolwich Station Museum which is housed in the original North Woolwich Station, built in 1854 and recently restored.

## Surrey Docks

Stretching along the south side of the Thames, from London Bridge to Rotherhithe and Downtown, existing Underground stations at London Bridge, Rotherhithe and Surrey Docks have contributed to the popularity of this sector and few vacant sites remained by the end of 1986. Unfortunately, as at Wapping, most of the great docks have been filled, only Canada Water, Greenland Dock and South Dock, all in the south-east section, surviving.

Occupying almost the entire river frontage between London Bridge and Tower Bridge is London Bridge City, a 2.5 million sq ft mixed development, one of Docklands' most important. It is best viewed from the river.

The Butlers Wharf scheme lies east of Tower Bridge and is easily approached from Shad Thames. Within this mixed development lies the Design Museum, transferred here from the Victoria and Albert Museum. Adjacent to Surrey Docks Underground station is the Surrey Quays Retail Centre (open October 1988), a £32 million shopping centre, Docklands' largest, which will rival North London's Brent Cross. Incorporated in the centre will be an 81,000 sq ft Tesco superstore and a 64,000 sq ft BHS department store.